Harbingers

Ashley J Horton

For those caught in between worlds
Those who thrive in the shadows
The witches, the gays, & the fae

<u>Hiraeth</u>

Noun

(especially in the context of Wales or Welsh culture)
deep longing for something, especially one's home.

Origin: Welsh/ of Celtic origin

(Oxford English Dictionary, 2021:online)

Prologue

The witch stood at her altar, three decks of tarot cards arranged on the wooden surface in front of her, candlelight flickered around her; as she thought to herself, where does my love lie? She shuffled the first deck and pulled a random tarot card out and sighed. She laid the High Priestess card on the altar, shuffling twice more pulling the Death and Fool card respectively. She set them next to the High Priestess. She placed the first deck back down on the altar and repeated the process with the other two decks, with the same results as the first deck; High Priestess, Death, Fool. She had known before she asked that she would pull these cards, she had pulled these same three cards for most of her adult life. Her love lies within herself as a witch, in her occupation as a death worker, and with her oblivious best friend who happened to be born on April Fool's Day. She sighed again and carefully wrapped her cards and put them away. Two out of three, she thought, and wondered idly if their lives would ever converge in a way where they could be together. Distance, work, and a myriad of other excuses seemed to always keep them physically apart, though they spoke daily.

"Something's gotta give…" She muttered to herself as she extinguished the lights and walked down the stairs leading out of her altar room.

At that exact moment, several hundred miles away, Fay, a modern day banshee, sat on the steps of a magnificent marble mausoleum. Her blond hair and pale skin appeared to be an extension of the moonlight she was bathed in. Shadowy images danced across her skin like the shadows on the moon's surface. She was smoking a clove and impatiently waiting. She had just started to burn a loose thread off her jeans when a big black crow with a peanut in his sleek, sharp beak landed next to her on the steps. She looked over and said, "You know, Bran, this harbinger of death shit is for the birds, no offense."

Bran cocked his head, one glistening black eye studying her, "Why would I take offense? It is for the birds." He paused, tilted his head the other way and said "and the sidhe," tilting his head again before looking down the path leading up to the mausoleum. "Oh, and the dogs." Just then a large black dog appeared on the path in front of them, as if from thin air.

Fay rolled her eyes and said, "Don't forget cats. Heck is impatiently waiting in the mausoleum. Come on Nubs it's almost dawn, it's time to go." With that she stood up, spun on her well-worn Doc Martens and walked through the mausoleum doors, Bran perched on her shoulder.

Anubis lumbered across the threshold growling and grumbling to himself, "I am named after the Egyptian God of Death and she calls me Nubs! No respect! I cannot help what happened to my tail..."

A low purring voice from somewhere inside the dark mausoleum stated, "I thought you worked it off." She dead panned. "You complain, yet she calls me Heck! Not Hecate goddess of magic, crossroads, and death..."

Just then Fay sighed, "because you're not."

"Are you sure, halfling?" Heck hissed.

"I mean, I'm pretty sure goddesses have thumbs." Fay smiled.

Heck glared gold slitted eyes at her, before turning back to her work. A small gold glow formed as Heck stood on her haunches and opened the portal, followed by darkness and silence as the harbingers took their leave.

The First of March

March 1

So, I woke up to the haunted antique Royal typewriter clicking clacking away at 3:33 am... I knew it was going to be a bad day. By the time I dragged myself into the living room (heh living room) Heck had just leapt up on the coffee table with a purring yawn. Nubs was sprawled on the couch. Bran was glaring at George, John, Paul, and Ringo, as the death watch beetles clicked anxiously awaiting our assignment. As soon as the typewriter stopped Heck hissed. Now what I asked her. She looked at me and said that we had been furloughed. I just looked at her with a blank, I've had too little sleep for this shit, stare. She repeated herself and I grabbed the note and read it aloud:

> Dear Harbinger Team NOLA,
>
> Due to a global pandemic, you are being placed on paid furlough until further notice. With the number of impending

deaths there will not be time, or enough harbingers, to warn all those whose death is imminent. Use this time to recharge as you will be busy again soon.

Stay safe my mortalish minions.

-Death Herself

Do you know what's more unsettling than the clicking of the deathwatch beetle? When the clicking stops and they become dead still and silent.

We were all silent for a moment and then I broke it like I do most things.

Yelling at no one in particular, "What the actual fuck is going on?"

Bran made some snarky remark about my verbal eloquence.

I flipped him the bird which brings me way more joy than it should, being that he's a crow.

Anyway, when you work for death, you never expect to get laid off because there's too much of it...

I have too many feelings...

I can't even right now.

-FF

After the harbingers sat, attempting to digest the information of now being on a forced vacation, Fay stood. She left the living room, walking with bare feet on worn hardwood floors straight back through the shotgun style house to the master bedroom, shutting the door behind her. Heck stood when she did and padded silently behind Fay, walking through the closed door to join her with a near inaudible hiss.

"Where are you going?" Heck asked.

"Who says I'm going anywhere?"

"Stop acting like I don't know you. You are headed to one of the cemeteries. Little things like hours of operations are of no consequence to death workers like us. Whether it's four in the morning or four in the evening, if you have something on your mind you are going to a cemetery. Which cemetery tells me your head space. If you head to Metairie, you are feeling contemplative or in need of your 'happy place', and you usually take a walk soaking in the scenery. If you go to Saint Roch, you are experiencing hiraeth and are going to sit amongst the prosthetic limbs in the chapel there and mourn your ghostly visage of wings. So, where are we going?"

"I am going to Saint Roch." Fay muttered, annoyed that the cat knew her so well.

"Ok, let's go."

Fay rolled her eyes, shoved her feet in her Docs, walked through the galley of a house, and out the front door. Heck close on her heels.

The Second of March

March 2

My wings, no more than phantoms on my back and a constant reminder of the homesickness I feel for a place I've never lived. So fucking painful some days.

At least I was granted the gift of veils. I've been holed up in the chapel at St. Roch for more than 24 hours. Not invisible, just unseen.

It truly is a mind fuck when death is your birthright (oh the irony) and to have your boss basically say, "your services are not needed at this time." It's like thanks, mom!

Because, yes, my boss, Death Herself, the most mysterious and unseen, fae is also my mother.

Also, a mind fuck to know death conceived you while reaping the soul of a human man.

I am birthed of death and now it's being taken away.

What am I to do with that?

What?

To not know your mother but miss her is confusing. To long for the Otherworld in which you have never lived is painful. To feel the wings that shimmer ghostly on your back in the right light, but are useless here, is torture.

I come here to this chapel when things weigh heavy, to remind myself that the humans, the other half of my being, experience this, when they lose a limb. I sit among the prosthetics of the dead to feel more human.

I'm glad Heck came with me. I can't ever tell her that. I'd never hear the end of it.

Fuckin' talking cats! Humans think it would be so cool. Yeah ok. They haven't had to deal with it for 33 years.

Marie, the previous banshee of New Orleans, now retired, (No not that Marie, though she is descended from the original Voodoo queen and banshee of New Orleans Marie Laveau. Well maybe that Marie, never mind I cannot fall down the reincarnation rabbit hole right now) raised me, and she says that Heck showed up on her doorstep 3

hours and 33 minutes after I was bestowed upon her, just after my

birth (another death/birth rabbit hole I cannot fall down right now)

I have a headache.

We should probably go home and leave these prostheses to rest.

-FF

Fay and Heck left the cemetery gates. She checked her phone and realized it was around lunch time, so she decided they would walk to Saint Roch Market and pick up some gumbo and crab cakes for her housemates. Everyone would pick at it except the beetles of course; they only ate wood.

When Fay checked her phone, she noticed a text from Jane McMortem, a death witch and banshee from Texas and she knew it was bad. All the text said was:

> **Did y'all receive notice?**

Yeah.

> **We were told that there would be so many near death**
>
> **that will recover, and others that won't.**
>
> **So, our presence would only cause panic and confusion.**

Wow. Ours was way more formal than that.

It basically read:

Your services are not

needed at this time.

> **Your mother really knows how**
>
> **to make her spawn feel special.**

Fay could literally feel the sarcasm drip from the text, but then again, that could just be the humidity in the air.

You home?

No, I've been at the cemetery ...

a while

Of course you have, St Roch?

Yeah

Oh, so you're super chipper.

Poor Heck.

Thanks for your concern...

for my cat.

So, have you heard what they're calling this thing?

No, what?

Dude!

You're gonna get a mouth full of angry feathers when you get home!

They're calling it Corvid 91!

They are basically calling it Crow Flu!

Fuck!

Yeah, I thought Merla was gonna pull her feathers out

She was so mad

Fuck.

Thanks for the heads up

I'm sure Bran will be super chill about this

No Prob

& good luck

Fay shoved her phone back into her ripped jeans, her long legs and Docs seeming heavier now. She sighed heavily and relayed her conversation with Jane to Heck, except for the part where Jane felt bad for Heck having to put up with her. Fay considered the idea that Jane and Heck might be in cahoots. She smiled a little and rolled her eyes fully at that thought.

The Third of March

March 3

Jane was right. When I got home there were feathers flying. Nubs had his head buried under his favorite pillow that says "Feliz Naughty dog" on it. He still won't let me pack it up. It's freaking March!

Bran was pacing both by wing and by foot while watching the news. He screeched something to the effect of "that will teach you to 'eat crow'." Have you ever seen a crow try to make quotations with his wings? It would have been hilarious if it hadn't been so frightening. Heck took one look at the crazed bird and excused herself with an "oh my" under her breath. I mean "oh my" pretty much sums it up. It's quite shocking to see a creature as old as New Orleans itself lose his shit... literally... all over the house. You know because crow shit and feathers all over the house makes everything better.

The news is talking about shutting everything down. There are very few times this city has shut its eyes and slept.

The last time was Katrina.

I was a young banshee then, still under the care of Marie, but I was here for that too.

Now that I'm thinking about it, we harbingers were shut down then too, after our initial warnings leading up to the hurricane that is. We were so busy comforting those injured or dying and helping clean up that it doesn't feel like we were "shut down."

-FF

The Fourth of March

March 4

I should have stayed at St Roch, as macabre as it is (this from a child

of death). It's way more peaceful than being in this house.

I may end up killing Bran, damn the consequences.

I ordered a roll of plastic sheeting, should be here tomorrow.

Bran is pacing the mantle.

Back and forth

Forth and back

Back and forth

Watching the news

And cawing, cursing, and crapping

Every time they refer to this virus as Corvid 91 he literally loses his shit all over again.

My poor furniture.

The beetles disappeared into the wisteria jungle never to be seen again, or at least not until we have a job to do.

Nubs keeps skulking out after dark and staying away until dawn. I can't blame him. He's taking this harder than Bran in some ways, I think. I've never really seen a grim eat, breathe, and sleep death quite like him.

No death worker really.

Death Herself probably takes more time off than Nubs.

Currently Heck and I are holed up in my room blaring, In This Moment, Garbage, Lindsey Stirling, Dresden Dolls, and any other music that we can agree on to drown out the chaos crow.

I don't know if we're all gonna to survive this.

Help.

-FF

The Fifth of March

March 5

Thank the gods; Hecate (not the cat), Venus, the Amazonian,

Nike (not the shoe), and whoever else.

The plastic sheeting was delivered today, so now my furniture is

protected from random acts of shit and feathers.

Seriously what the fuck, bird!?

Ugh.

He either needs to go see Merla or she needs to come and calm

his corvid ass down before he loses all his feathers.

I politely (for me) asked him if maybe it would be better to NOT

watch the news ALL the time.

He did not like this!

He feels someone should be informed and I clearly don't care enough.

I glared at him and asked what he's learned in the last 24 hours, other than it's apparently birdly possible (instead of humanly (I don't know why he hates me sometimes)) for him to continue shitting everywhere after exhausting all his stores.

He did not like this either.

He puffed up at me. Clearly, he feels I was being flippant. He's not shitting on HIS furniture mind you.

I smiled at him and told him he was the prettiest.

He gawked at me speechless, so I walked away while there was silence.

One day he will get it.

Or maybe one day I will tell him.

-FF

The Sixth of March

March 6

Marie called today.

We talked for a while.

She finds my predicament with Bran quite amusing.

I reminded her that it's because she doesn't live here anymore. In fact as I see it Bran is hers. Bran belonged to the original Marie and then came to this Marie on her 13th birthday. Since Marie is still alive, and she gifted him to me, he is mine until the next incarnation of Marie is born. She only "gifted" him because he's involved with Merla and likes the work we do. I know he pops over to San Diego to see her and Marie's cat Voodoo at least once a week.

She said things are already strict in San Diego she said, and I quote, "But it don't bother me none. My retirement goes on as planned, they may see Mama Marie's footsteps in the sand, but I was gone before they spared a glance."

I chuckled at that, that woman doesn't give a fuck about what people may think. I'm not sure if that's her own attitude or the voodoo queen's, but I suspect both.

Then the conversation turned to me (super).

She said to me then, "So much of your young life has been spent workin' one way or another. Mama Marie wants ya to focus on what you love during this time."

Yeah, okay old lady. Whatever that means.

For what it's worth I've spent the last several hours by myself, editing photographs I took at Metairie, I love that place. It's so beautiful and peaceful there.

Flotsam even let me take a few of him. It's truly an honor to have a faery creature trust you enough to capture him in his home. Those are my favorites to date. He's a special guy and a good friend. I can't wait to show him the final images.

Other than my photography that falls by the wayside when work is busy, I'm not sure what else Mama Marie could mean.

-FF

Fay finished writing and was tucking her battered notebook back into her shoulder bag when her phone sang three words, *living dead girl*. Anytime she heard the Rob Zombie hit it made her think of Jane; well, it made her think of all banshees, but when her phone sang it, she knew it was Jane. She picked up her phone smiling.

Hey, been a couple days… how's things?

A mess. Bran literally lost his shit

ALL OVER THE HOUSE

Despite your warning

I was NOT prepared for his drama

It looks like things may shut down

Reminds me of Katrina.

Geez Katrina, that was so hard

We were awfully young then

Yeah 18 and 20 if memory serves.

Wee baby banshees.

That tragedy brought our teams together,

so it wasn't all bad.

Fay sent the text and reached for her cup, which proclaimed the contents to be Luminol, and took a drink.

Yes, quite the love story from our teams' encounters.

Fay choked on her drink when she read that, and then another text came in.

> **Just ask the love birds themselves.**
>
> **Speaking of that, Merla mentioned**
>
> **she's trying to get Bran to come here**
>
> **That should ease the tension and cleaning issues at your house.**

Once Fay could breathe again, she texted:

I apologize to you and your furniture

in advance of Bran's arrival. RIP

She added a headstone emoji for good measure.

> **Is the headstone for my couch or Bran when I kill him?**

Yes.

At least if you kill him

He will have a proper burial

Maybe you should ask his preference

> **that will go over well**

Fay sat her phone down and shook her head. Jane and she met fifteen years ago in the aftermath of Katrina, both comforting the dying. A little known fact about banshees (because they are rarely 'seen' when working other than by the dying and very sensitive) is that not only do they warn of impending death, but can also comfort the dying in their final moments. Those who have seen them, call them the angels of death. Fay stayed with the dying people her presence calming them, and Jane did the same for the animals. They became fast and sometimes flirty friends, but that's it. The crows, however, have been inseparable ever since, spending any free time together either in New Orleans or Austin. Fay sighed, stood up to go find Bran and see if he took the Austin team up on their offer to go fuck up their house.

Fay found Bran sitting on the coffee table, seemingly calm but puffed up. When he was puffed up like that it reminded her of a Mardi Gras Indian, but she kept that right where it belonged, in her head. He waited for Heck to open a portal for him. Although the harbingers had the ability to open portals for themselves for travel, cats were more adept at it and could do so for others using little energy. Heck sat up on her haunches batting at the air as if at an unseen insect, and a soft glow began to form about the size for a crow to fit in. Bran hopped through without a word. Once Bran was gone the glow dissipated, Heck sat back down and looked at Fay a little cross eyed, shook her head and said, "Hey, what's up."

"I'm thinking about walking to the quarter and see how the city feels. Think I may stop at Erin Rose for a frozen Irish coffee, want to come with?" Fay asked.

"I want to go." Nubs said lumbering in, now that the crazed crow had vacated.

"Ok, but you have to wear the leash."

"Ugh, fine. It's so undignified" He groaned.

"I'll wear a leash too, if that makes you feel better." Heck offered.

Nubs' ears perked a little and he said, "It does."

Fay rolled her eyes and went and grabbed the leashes. She knew no one would look twice at a giant shaggy black dog and a small black cat both on leashes in her city.

The Seventh of March

March 7

It's late or early.

I spent the evening wandering the quarter with Heck and Nubs,

checking the pulse of the city.

I found it pitter pattering like that of the hunted or perhaps the

haunted.

We started at Erin Rose and I chatted with the bartenders as I drank

my Irish coffee. There are rumbling of closings and fears because

Mardi Gras was just a couple weeks ago and there were SO MANY

PEOPLE. Before I left I got an Irish coffee to go. Once we were around

the corner from the bar I put the Irish coffee on the ground for Heck

and Nubs.

For being these supposedly dignified harbingers of death, they are total sluts for frozen Irish coffee.

I find Nubs to be an interesting study, he is the picture of Scottish nobility, always looking wise and aloof. However, when Irish coffee is involved, he gets the goofiest smile (grims have the best smiles) on his Deerhound face. All the grims look like Scottish Deerhounds, large and lanky with shaggy wavy fur, and great beards. Instead of a gray tone to their fur they have varying shades of black fur, Nubs is no different. I think he may take his status a bit more seriously than other grims, which is why it's such a delight when he comes down from his pedestal to hang out with us lesser beings.

Heck acts like a kitten hyped up on catnip as she laps up Irish coffee. It's ridiculous!

I can't help but smile at them; sometimes it really is the small things.

From Erin Rose we walked down Conti to Royal, I went to NOLA4EVER, where my friend Jen is a shopkeeper. She too was as unsettled as the bartenders at Erin Rose. She knelt on the sidewalk to lavish both Heck and Nubs with love (sluts) and told me she has heard muttering of closures not just here but state and country wide.

I told her vaguely that I had a friend in Texas updating me on their situation and it's not great. After that we walked down Royal toward Jackson Square and stopped at The Corner Oyster Bar. I tied the precious wuv wuvs, as Jen had called them, to a post outside with some water. They glared at me while I sat chatting with Batgirl (she has bats tattooed behind her ear, she also has tentacles running down her arm, but I thought Batgirl sounded better than Squidgirl. I think her name is Melissa) at the bar. I slurped down some oysters and ordered some beignet fries with banana fosters sauce to share with Mr & Mrs. McGlare outside. Batgirl's feelings were also of impending doom in the city.

I was feeling quite subdued as we walked through the sea of fortune tellers outside Saint Louis Cathedral. I wondered idly if any of them had seen this coming.

Once we got to the mostly vacant Pirates Alley I had Heck portal us home, I didn't feel like walking anymore.

When we got home, I texted Jane to see how Bran was.

All I got back was a picture of a Mardi Gras Indian.

I smirked and told her about how defeated the city felt.

Now to bed.

-FF

Fay slept fitfully that night, a medley of messed up scenes. Black wispy bat wings disappearing into the shadows, the faces of the dying she's touched, feathers raining from the sky, the sound of every banshee in the world wailing at once, the sun exploding, the moon crumbling, so much panic... and purring?

Then there was her face, her kind and soothing green eyes, a fiery red mane of hair that smelled of sage and roses. Her voice whispering, "Wake up."

Fay sat straight up in her bed breathing hard as her phone sang *Living Dead Girl.*

She searched her bed for her phone, under the pillow, because that's obviously where it goes.

"You should invite her here." Heck said.

"Holy shit! How long have you been sitting there?"

"Long enough to know you were having a panicked dream and long enough to know when Jane came into the dream."

"Were you peeping?" Fay glared at the cat.

"I don't have to, and you should still invite her here."

"What, why?"

"You are so dense." Heck chuffed.

"I am too tired for..." just then Fay's phone went off again. She checked the message.

You up?

Have you seen the news?

Shutting down New Orleans, I bet it's gonna be eerie.

Fay looked up at Heck, "Have you seen the news?"

"Yes." Heck hissed.

"And you want me to invite her to a locked down city? For what? To look at all the great bars and restaurants we can't eat in?"

"You are impossible!"

"Me? I can't with you... I need coffee..."

"Well, you're gonna have to make it yourself. No thumbs, remember?"

Heck stood up, turned and stretched languorously, allowing her tail to linger in Fay's face before she jumped down and sauntered out into the hallway, leaving Fay sitting alone, grumpy, and groggy in her bedroom. Fay remembered her phone. Picked it up and hastily tapped out a text:

I'm awake now

The CAT not only informed me

of the city's doom

But that I would have to

make my own coffee

due to lack of thumbs on her part.

Well, that sounds like a pleasant way to wake up

Does it now?

You wanna come see how pleasant it is?

Fay sent the text before she realized what she had written. Then it

dawned on her and she whispered to herself a mantra of, "Fuck!

Fuck! Fuck! Fuuuuck!" And then her phone buzzed in her hand.

Is that an invitation?

Jane texted back with a winky emoji.

Fay's mantra started up all over again, "Fuck! Fuck!..."

Heck strode in and asked, "What's all the fucking

about!"

Fay glared at her and showed her the phone.

"Oh my, you actually did it!" Heck said in slight disbelief.

"I... I didn't me... yeah... fuck!" Fay blathered out.

"Well, you better say something. Probably not fuck though."

"Thanks, oh wise thumbless cat."

"You're welcome, oh dense deathling," Heck left the room again with what appeared to be a smirk on her cat face.

Fay picked up her phone again, stared for another second and texted:

It is, if you want it to be.

She hit send and started her mantra again with what felt like moths flittering in her stomach and chest, "Fuck, fuck, fuck!"

Her phone buzzed again.

Ok, let me see what I need to wrap up here

I suspect I'll have a lot of down time.

Call you later.

Ok, cool.

Fay let out a breath she had no idea she had been holding and fell dramatically back on her pillow.

She spent the rest of the day trying to enjoy the calm in her house and ignore the self-induced panic in her head. Heck and Nubs thoroughly enjoyed the calm and lounged in the living room all day. Heck slept with an oddly smug look on her kitty face.

The Eighth of March

March 8

Fuck!

Apparently, I have invited Jane to come stay with me and explore New Orleans during the shutdown.

What was I thinking?!?

I wasn't, clearly.

She called me last night to say she can come tomorrow evening.

She needs to tie up some loose ends and make sure her apprentice will be at the pet cemetery and crematory she owns. She said she would have to portal back at least once a week to take care of things there, but otherwise she's free to explore New Orleans with me.

I'm so excited and nauseous all at once.

It looks like some restaurants will be open for to-go, so we can eat,

and our skill sets will allow us entry into places most cannot enter.

Deep breaths Fay

DEEP BREATHS!

Fuck!

-FF

Fay forced herself out of bed as a fresh wave of panic at what she had done yesterday slammed into her. She made coffee and began scanning the rooms of the house making sure everything was in order, hoping she hadn't missed any feathers or bird shit. The thought of feathers triggered the memory of the dream she woke from yesterday morning. She shook her head, poured her coffee, and went out the side door in the kitchen, to go sit quietly out in her wisteria jungle of a backyard. She sat in her old paint chipped and rusty vintage deck chair and watched the bees buzz through the wild wisteria. She couldn't quite remember her dreams from last night; her mind wandered until she lost herself completely in watching the bees. So much so that she didn't even notice when Heck walked through the closed back door and hopped up in the chair next to hers.

"What is wrong with you?"

Fay startled and glanced at her, "I don't know."

"You two have known each other since 2005! She's your best friend. I mean she's your only human friend, but that's not the point."

"Is this your idea of a fucking pep talk? Promise me you'll never work a suicide hotline."

Heck sat up on her haunches, "No thumbs, remember? I just don't understand why you're being weirder than normal."

"I don't know, we haven't hung out in person since Katrina, I don't really think that was hanging out. Plus, our work has always kept us busy until now. What if we're awkward face to face? It's different via text and phone calls."

"Yeah, somehow I don't think that's gonna be an issue, except… for the crush you have on her, that could make it weird, if you act weird around her."

Fay choked on the coffee she was drinking, "The what?" She gasped trying to suck in air and not coffee.

Heck scoffed and jumped from the chair, "You heard me, halfling." She then sauntered through the still closed door leaving Fay in stunned silence.

The Ninth of March

March 9

Jane will be here in a couple of hours, around 6 PM I think, and I've clearly lost my goddamn mind. My hair which normally lays straight down my back has puffed in this fucking humidity. I have changed my outfit three times like the woman hasn't seen me knee deep in muck. What the fuck is wrong with me?

Why do I care what I am wearing? We're probably just gonna hang around the house tonight.

I have finally decided on a mint green shirt that says "I wanna give you the creeps" with a headstone on it, my ripped and faded blue jeans and my black platform zip-up Docs.

Why do I need my Docs on one might ask?

Docs= comfort X security

WHAT IS WRONG WITH ME!?

Ugh. I look hideous.

Wraith like with my bedraggled hair

Why am I wasting time writing?

I'm gonna go straighten my hair...

Again.

-FF

Fay paced through the shotgun style house from her master suite, passed the guest entrance to the bathroom, into the kitchen, through the small dining area and into the living room and back again. She alternated running her hands through her hair and flexing her hands as she paced. Nubs and Heck watched from the couch.

Finally, Heck spoke, "Oh my gods, you need a fidget spinner or something! If you don't stop pacing, we are going to have to have the floors refinished. You are wearing them out."

"Whatever." Fay glared and turned expertly on her docs and began to pace back from the living room to her room. Just as she stepped a pale green glow lit up behind her as Jane and her cat, Mr. Ebisneezer Snooze, a white and ginger long hair with severe allergy issues, appeared in the light. The light dissipated, Ebisneezer stood there looking a little cross eyed and sneezed. Fay turned back around staring at the woman and cat now standing in her living room, really taking them in (well, her in). Jane stood there looking confident though her face betrayed her nervousness for a brief second. Her blazing wavy hair was shoulder length and all combed to the left side of her head exposing a shaved right side. She wore gray jeans, a green long sleeved paisley peasant style shirt, and gray high heeled Docs. Her green eyes smiled as she took Fay in. When Fay remembered that she could in fact speak English she said, "Hey, glad y'all could come." In her head she thought, oh my gods stop gawking and being so awkward.

"Me too," Jane said. "What better place to be if the world's ending than one of the most superstitious and haunted cities in the world." She laughed.

Fay's tension eased with Jane's laugh, and she said, "Your hair looks awesome, when did you change it? It was longer in the last photo you sent."

Jane blushed, "Oh good. It looks intentional then?" She looked a little self-conscious and continued, "long story short, I was working on a new spell today and well... it backfired. So I had to improvise with my hair. Luckily, I am good with hair."

"Do I even want to know? Never mind. Your hair looks great. So wipe whatever that look is off your face and follow me. I'll give you the grand tour of my not so grand house." Jane smiled and set her stuff by the couch and followed Fay through the house. "The room you are departing is the living room, as you can see there are creatures living in it. Now you've entered the small dining area, where Heck and I gaze into each other's eyes across the table."

"Glare!" Heck yelled from the living room, "not gaze."

Next to the window stood a small black stained wood table and two chairs with wine red seat cushions, one clearly covered in black fur.

"And over here on this wall is an altar to the ancestors of landlines past." There in the wall was a telephone nook with an unplugged rotary phone, with the headset off the hook and unplugged from the phone base. Burned candles melted to the surface surrounding it.

"Why…?" Jane began

"Is the phone off the hook and unplugged?"

Jane nodded.

"Because I thought this would be a fun piece until we started getting phantom calls. Like literal phantoms! Ghosts calling at all hours. The phone rang several times a day, and I don't have a landline. So, measures were taken."

"The candles? Were they part of the scene you were setting or part of the measures?" Jane asked curiously.

"Yes." Fay answered.

Jane chuckled and as they headed through the house, she noticed all the walls were painted the same color of stormy gray while the ceilings were different, always deep colors. The living room ceiling was dark teal, the dining room was a deep red that matched the cushions on the chairs. As she walked into the small kitchen, she noticed the ceiling was a metallic looking purple. She couldn't help but wonder what color Fay's bedroom ceiling would be. They exited the kitchen into a tiny hallway that had two doors, but felt like there had once been three.

"Here is the guest entrance to the shared bathroom. Back here used to be two bedrooms but I remodeled it into one once Marie retired and I took over the house. They walked into the bathroom first and it caught Jane by surprise. This was the only room thus far without gray walls. The walls were black, pink, and brown. Fay was looking at her with a mischievous grin.

"What?" Jane asked.

"That look, the pure consternation and confusion. It's what I was going for here. Everything thus far in the house has been calm, dark and bold, then you walk in here and well, your face says it all."

"Yeah, I feel a little like I've been slapped in the face."

"Exactly."

The bathroom was done in a black and gray pinstriped wallpaper with large brown moths and pink roses. "Are those moths?" Jane asked.

"Yes!" Fay's smile brightened. "The brown and beige accent tiles around the tub area and sink are original, and ugly, but original. I didn't want to get rid of them, so I found a wallpaper that would incorporate the color into my reimagined bathroom. I had the bathroom gutted except for the original tile. Putting in a black sink, toilet, and the clawfoot. I could have had the clawfoot all black, but it was too much like sinking into a swamp, so that's why the exterior is black, and the interior is white. I also made sure there was a stand-alone shower for when Marie visits. She loathes a bath, and I knew she wouldn't be comfortable showering in the clawfoot. I chose the black hexagon tiles for the floor. All the accents and the ceiling are the same pink in the roses on the wallpaper. I'm fairly sure this mirror is haunted, so be careful looking in it. It can appear a little crowded in here some days."

There, above the sink, hung a gaudy ornate mirror painted pink.

"Well... I'm glad my response was what you were looking for. As for the mirror, a portal is a portal, is a portal haunted or not." She said, watching wisps drift in and out of view. " So... Is your bedroom this much of a mind fuck?"

"I don't know, I guess that depends on how you feel about cemeteries."

"Well, as you know, I'm quite the fan"

They ventured forth through the bathroom door leading into the master. Jane held in a gasp as they walked into Fay's room. It was beautiful. The walls were the same gray as the rest of the house, but the ceiling in the large room was a midnight blue with what appeared to be glitter in it. The king bed was encased in ornate wrought iron. There was a large canvas above the head that read *At Rest.* The walls had massive canvases with photographs of cemetery statues on them. The windows though were breathtaking. There were three of them, all arched stained glass windows. The one that faced the side of the house depicted an above ground tomb with a crow sitting atop it and a pale girl walking toward it. There were two facing the back of the house. One was mostly blue, a night sky with the moon lighting up a tomb. The third one was different, and Jane eyed it carefully. It was a young blond girl, and if she didn't know better she would have thought the girl was wearing combat boots, with a crow perched on her shoulder, a black cat to her left, and a black dog to her right, sitting almost as tall as the girl. As Fay walked up Jane glanced down at her Docs and back up at the window smiling.

Fay stood behind Jane watching her look at the window. "That one," she said softly, "is older than the rest. This corner over here," Fay gestured to an area that encompassed the window, a desk, computer, cameras, and accessories, "was my room when I was younger. Marie had the window custom made for me for my 13th birthday. I had the other two commissioned when Marie moved out and I redid the room."

"I see some things never change." Jane gestured toward Fay's shoes.

"What can I say? I like what I like, to the chagrin of Heck and Marie both I'm afraid." She grinned and continued, "The bed, I had a friend rework the welding from fencing around a couple of dilapidated tombs they were redoing after Katrina. The photographs are my work."

"The photographs are yours? Wow, I know you've texted me your work before and have talked about setting up in Jackson Square when the death game is slow, but our phones do not do them justice! These are fucking magnificent." Her eyes fixed on the huge photographs.

"Thanks." Fay grumbled and blushed a little. "So, this is my house that I share with a bunch of death omens. You can crash on the couch, it pulls out, but it may smell… grim." Her eyes twinkled for a moment as the pun rolled off her tongue, "I have an air mattress I can pull out of the closet. The bed is also plenty big. I have a coffin shaped body pillow somewhere I can put in the middle as a barrier if you like."

"Of course, you do." Jane said, rolling her eyes. "Bed's fine. Coffin not necessary." She walked from the bedroom and said, "What does the outside look like? I just portaled in, so I have no idea." Fay smiled as she walked to catch up with Jane showing her out the side door and into the wisteria jungle. From there they walked out the front gate together and crossed the street to look at the house.

"Of course, it is." Jane said, staring at Fay in disbelief. The shotgun style house was sandwiched between a lavender house and a mint green house. Fay's house was a pebble gray color with black trim and shutters, with white ginger breading that looked like spiderwebs.

"Whhhat?" Fay said in faux innocence.

"Really?"

Fay looked at Jane very seriously and said, "Well, Jane, death lives here."

Jane rolled her eyes and walked across the street calling back, "Obviously Fay, anyone can see that." Gesturing dramatically with her hands.

Fay grinned and followed Jane back into the house. Jane sat on the couch along the side wall and Fay curled up in her oversized chair near an ornately covered useless fireplace.

"Why the fireplace?" Jane asked.

"I honestly don't know; I've lived here my whole life and I think we've used it three times. Plus, when you do use it, people call emergency services because they think your house is on fire."

Jane laughed, "That's wild! So, what's the plan?"

"Well, I figured we could just chill this evening, I know you want to see the cemeteries, I figured we would start with Saint Louis #1 and maybe #2, then we can walk through the quarter toward Jackson Square and see if there's anything open serving food and have a private picnic since everything, including Jackson Square, is shutting down."

"That sounds perfect."

Fay smiled, "Let me grab a couple ciders, we can sit on the stoop and people watch."

The two women sat outside chatting into the wee

hours of the morning, while Heck and Ebs sat in the window

watching, looking smug.

56

The Tenth of March

Fay woke the next morning curled up in her chair in the living room. Jane was still crashed out on the couch with Ebs asleep above her. Fay grabbed her phone that had slid from her pocket into the cushion and checked the time.

"Holy shit." She muttered. And then internally, *how is it almost eleven? When was the last time I slept this late? Hell, when was the last time I was up that late? What time did we come inside three, four? Who knows?*

"Y'all passed out around four in the morning." Heck whispered in Fay's ear.

"Goddammit, cat!" Fay hissed.

Just then Jane stirred, "Are y'all arguing about the logistics of making coffee without thumbs?" She yawned and smiled at them. Ebs lifted his head groggily, opening only one eye.

"I'm sure that's where this conversation was leading. These lovely morning interactions with Heck are what you really came for, right?" Fay smiled sardonically at Jane then turned and glared at the cat next to her.

"Not the only thing." Jane winked and let that linger there.

Without a word, Fay unfolded herself from the chair padding into the kitchen to make coffee. Heck came in behind her imparting her unwelcomed and never asked for wisdom, "You're an idiot." Then she walked through the wall and out into the wisteria jungle.

A few minutes later Jane appeared in the kitchen, following the smell of chicory. Fay turned and handed her a cup. "I was thinking I would make some peanut butter and banana toast, interested?"

"Depends."

"On?"

"If you have honey, of course."

Fay rolled her eyes and pulled a honey bear out of the

cabinet, setting it on the counter, "Of course I have honey. What kind of person doesn't have honey?" She then busied herself making toast. They ate at the small table together in mostly sleepy silence. When they finished Jane retrieved her bag from the living room, disappearing into the bathroom, while Fay dressed in her room. Fay was sitting in the chair in the living room when Jane reappeared.

"Ready?" Fay asked as she stood picking up a camera bag.

"Yes!" Jane said with a glint of excitement in her eye.

Both cats were magically at their feet, Ebs opening a portal for them.

As soon as their feet touched cemetery soil there was a faery creature in Jane's face, and both cats disappeared.

"Who are you!" The small but fierce creature said, shoving a ridiculously small but very real sword in her face.

"Greetings Dartanya, it's great to see that you are still fiercely protective of this excellent cemetery." Fay said "she's with me."

The faery's features softened, "Fay, I didn't see you there!"

"Yes, I know. I promise you; no harm will come to you or this cemetery by myself or my friend here."

With that, Dartanya sheathed her sword, flitted a little closer, stuck out her hand and said, "Hello, I am Dartanya, faery protector, taphofae, and guardian of Saint Louis Cemetery #1." She puffed out her chest as she finished shaking Jane's finger. Then she flitted over and sat on Fay's shoulder. Looking at Fay she said, "it's been incredibly quiet here since the decree, very few people, and those that have been entering, other than the grounds keeper, have meant harm, so I've been on high alert."

"Yes, we can see the high alert. Why don't you go rest a bit, I can keep an eye out while we wander, and I'll let you know before we leave."

Dartanya nodded and flitted away and through a crack in one of the wall vaults.

The two began to walk. "I do not envy her. She must be the most vigilant of the taphofae because of the history of this cemetery.

Only tours and families of the deceased are allowed in, but it doesn't mean others don't try. At one point, while Dartanya was visiting her family in the Otherside, vandals painted the family tomb of Marie Laveau pink. She will never forgive herself for that one. I wasn't sure Marie was going to forgive her either; it took forever to restore. Over here is the one day final resting place of a famous Hollywood actor."

"It's a pyramid!"

"It's that, and an eye sore. I'm clearly not the only one who thinks so." Fay said looking up, "It's been struck by lightning twice." She looked back at Jane, "Wait til you see the Brunswig Mausoleum at Metairie. It puts this pyramid to shame."

"Please don't hold back your true feelings." Jane said before getting distracted, "Oh, what's that about?" Jane said, pointing to a dilapidated tomb covered in X's, Mardi Gras beads, bottles of booze, trinkets, cigarettes, and coins.

"That is one of the many false tombs of Marie Laveau. Well, it is and it isn't. According to Marie, there are descendants entombed throughout the cemetery, that's one of them. The original voodoo queen is buried in the family tomb over here, which is kept in pristine condition. Especially after the painting fiasco. Based on Marie's age I would say she is the second incarnation of the voodoo queen, whether or not there was a Marie before the Maries I don't know. Do you have a headache now? I think I do."

Jane just looked at her a little wide eyed and smiled.

They walked companionably, Fay pointing out things of interest and answering Jane's questions. As they were rounding a corner Jane noticed a lavender arrow painted in the path.

"Well, that seems different, even for here." she said.

Fay pointed at it and said" follow it!"

Jane followed where the arrow was pointing and saw a wall vault painted the same color lavender. "Whoa," she said.

"Sometimes people paint the tombs to match the color of the house." Fay informed her.

"That's really cool!" Jane said and then started laughing.

"What?" Fay asked.

"Well, two things, your neighbor's house is lavender, do you know this family? Secondly, I just imagined you having a tomb painted all black and gray and spiderwebby, and it should go next to this one."

Fay glared at her playfully and said, "Come on, let's find Dartanya and get out of here."

Just then both cats and Dartanya appeared from thin air. "Ready?" Heck asked.

Fay gave her a sideways look, "Yeah, but you already knew that."

"Ok, where to?" Heck asked, ignoring Fay's insinuation.

"I think we will do Saint Louis #2 another day, the dead are not going anywhere." Fay said smiling at Jane, "So just to the corner of North Rampart and St. Peter. I think walking through the quarter will be interesting."

"Ok."

One moment they were standing at the gates of the cemetery, the next they were standing at the corner of St. Peter.

They walked down St. Peter all the way to Royal noticing just how empty the quarter really was. There were residents out on stoops and balconies soaking in the relative silence of it all. There were some homeless in the doorways of closed-up shops. Fay pointed out a few places along the way.

"That's Boondock Saint. They always have the movie playing on a small TV above the bar."

"Really?" Jane asked.

"Yeah, I wouldn't be surprised if it wasn't playing now even with it all closed up. We could go check if you want."

"Nah, I believe you."

"I'm sure you do, but what's the point of having the ability to portal and veil and not use them for fun once in a while?"

Jane rolled her eyes, "Maybe we should save B & E for my next visit; besides... I'm getting hungry."

"Sure, next time." Fay said with an exaggerated wink. "Well, if you can't make it the few more blocks to Corner we can stop at Rouses and pick up some snacks."

Jane rolled her eyes again, "I can make it."

They walked a couple more minutes before arriving at a side door with a table blocking it. Batgirl was there taking orders.

"Hey." Fay said.

"Hey! You made it just in time. This is it; we're closing completely after today." Batgirl exclaimed.

"Oh no! What will I do without beignet fries and banana foster sauce." Fay sighed dramatically faux fainting.

Smiling, Batgirl shook her head, "Perish, I suspect."

"Probably. Well, can I get an order for old times' sake, and speaking of perish, what do you have the most of that you need to get rid of?"

"I still got quite a bit of gumbo, and shrimp Creole, I've also got a lot of bread so I can do some po'boys."

"Ok, give me a couple orders of each, last me a little while before I go into complete withdrawal. What are y'all doing with what's left?"

"Probably give it to the homeless, it's like they can sense it, and are lining up."

"Yeah, there seems to be quite a lot of homeless down

this way, didn't see as many in the other end of the quarter."

Fay and Jane stepped out of the way and let other people order while they waited for their food. When Batgirl let them know their food was ready she handed them an extra bag with po'boys in it, she asked if they wouldn't mind handing them out to the homeless on the other side of the quarter. They agreed and turned to leave. Fay walked right into someone upon turning.

"Oh shit, I am so sorry." She said to a beard, long trench coat, and top hat.

"No worries, lass." The trench coat said

She backed up a few steps and focused, "Oh, hey Wolf. It's been a while."

"It has indeed, lass. Who is your friend?"

"Oh sorry! Wolf, this is Jane, she is a death worker in Texas."

"Ah, nice to meet you, Jane. I am one of the New Orleans area reapers."

"Nice to meet you, as well."

"Well, we are going to sneak into Jackson Square and

eat." Fay said.

"Enjoy lassies, Jackson Square when it's closed is my favorite place to prowl."

The cats appeared at their sides near the gates of Jackson Square and portaled them in. Fay gave the extra food to the cats and asked them to distribute it on the other side of the quarter. The cats portaled away and the two women walked to the statue of Andrew Jackson and sat down at the base and began unloading tons of food. They ate and Fay talked a little about the history.

"So much history has happened right here. It was originally called Place d'Armes by the French, it has seen battles, and been the place of public executions."

"It's so beautiful though."

"It is, though I wouldn't be caught dead here after dark, except for maybe around Christmas time. The spirits play out their histories and it can be quite overwhelming, especially around Halloween. A couple weeks before Christmas they have caroling here and it's pretty amazing, this coming from someone who hates Christmas. You have locals, tourists, and spirits all singing in harmony. The living holding candles and the spirits bask in the glow. It seems to calm the spirits for a little while at least."

"I would love to see that."

"Then I guess you better be here on the third Sunday in December."

"It's a date." Jane said before shoving half a po'boy in her mouth.

They finished eating, walked around the square for a bit, just before dark Heck and Ebs reappeared and portaled them home.

March 10

It's just before midnight. This is the first free moment I've had to write.

Jane is asleep in my bed. In. my. bed.

Today was incredible despite the comatose pulse of the city.

Being the awkward person that I am, and spending most of my time talking to a cat, I wasn't really sure I would be able to talk to her in person. I know it sounds dumb even writing it, but texting someone daily for years and jumping straight into an open ended sleepover is kinda extreme. It would seem that the texts translated well.

Today we went to St.Louis #1, and boy was Dartanya feisty.

Apparently taphofae in Austin are a lot more chill like Matthew McConaughey . They're like alright alright alright come right on in the cemetery.

The entire quarter is pretty much closing down. Places are being boarded up.

It looks like the storm of the century is heading toward the city.

Maybe it is.

I literally ran into Wolf this evening. Ugh, so embarrassing.

We were leaving Corner when I turned around right into him. So dumb, he was quite gracious about it all. I introduced him to Jane, in a broad sense. I find it weird introducing death workers to each other; it always reminds me of a bad joke or something.

A witch, a banshee, and a reaper go into a bar...

I've clearly started to ramble.

Anyway, he was out doing his rounds through the homeless. He always seems so compassionate towards them, helping those he can, reaping those he can't.

Ok, well I guess... I'm off to bed.

The bed that Jane is already in. My bed.

I do not know how I've managed not being completely awkward in person, when I am clearly awkward in my own private writings.

Goodnight cringe worthy me,

-FF

The Eleventh of March

Fay woke up startled, having momentarily forgotten there was another woman in her bed. When she first opened her cloudy blue eyes and saw Jane sitting there she was confused, then she remembered, but then she really looked at Jane and was confused all over again. Jane was sitting cross legged in the bed, her right elbow braced on her leg, her head resting on her palm, eyes closed. Her messy red hair draped like curtains down the front of her face. Her other hand rested on her left leg, palm up cell phone resting on the palm. Every so often she would grasp the phone and blindly tap something out. Fay debated whether she should stay, as to not disturb her, or if she should quietly get out of bed and leave the room to give her some privacy. Just as she slowly and quietly turned to crawl out of her side of the bed, a hand reached out and gently but firmly grabbed her wrist.

"Please don't go. It is your bed after all." Jane said.

Fay turned back toward Jane and said, "Ok, I didn't want to disturb you or intrude on a private moment."

Jane laughed a little, "I would, for sure, be an asshole if I was mad at you for intruding on a private moment, not just in your house, but in your bed!"

"Well, I can't argue with that. Are you ok, though?"

"Yes, I'm not used to having a human audience for a download, but yes, I'm fine. The universe sends me a mental download of all the animals that are about to cross. Usually, it's only the animals that will be coming into my care, but sometimes I get to know when my friends and relatives animals are gonna cross. Fun trick, right? It's why I'm so popular at parties." She turned her head smiling brightly at Fay.

"Wow, you go to parties? What's that like?" Fay snarked. Followed in a more serious tone, "I'm honored to be the rare human-like creature to witness this download."

"Human-like?" Jane began and quickly continued "Oh yeah, that's right I forgot, literal child of death."

"That's me." Fay said with faux pride, stabbing herself in the chest with both thumbs.

Jane rolled her eyes, "Unfortunately, this download means I'm gonna have to go back to Austin soon for a couple of days."

"Oh. When?" Fay asked, feeling inexplicably bummed.

"Probably tomorrow evening. I like to start my workings at night. They will be crossing soon, though their physical bodies will not arrive for a couple days yet." Jane hesitated suddenly feeling shy and asked, "Would you... want to come to Austin with me?"

"Yes!" Fay almost shouted, then more calmly, "yes, I would love to. I've never seen a witch at work. Is that even allowed? With all the cloak and dagger secrecy."

"It's not, actually. My apprentice and I are gonna blindfold you, spin you around a couple times, and walk you backwards so you have no idea what's going on, then we're gonna make a bunch of wild shit up since you can't see."

Fay grinned at her teasing and said, "Well, that sounds fun too."

Jane shook her head and put her phone up as they both got out of bed in search of coffee, "Oh and it's called an athame, not a dagger." Jane said with a wry smile.

Once they had a sufficient amount of caffeine in their systems and had each eaten a granola bar, they gathered their things. Fay didn't even bother with her cameras this time, she was too busy playing tour guide.

"So, I thought we could portal ourselves to the Warehouse District, giving the cats a day off." She glared down the hall where she could sense Heck listening and continued, "and ride the streetcar from there all the way to the end where it literally dead ends at the cemeteries. Greenwood will be the most noticeable from the streetcar, it has a hobbit hole like mausoleum with a giant elk on top. There are a bunch of cemeteries there including The Charity Hospital Cemetery which has a Katrina memorial. There's Oddfellow's Rest which is always closed, not that that's an issue. There is a headstone in there that makes me laugh, and around the corner a little ways is Holt Cemetery, which I find to be the most hauntingly beautiful and sad cemetery I've ever walked through."

"That's a lot!"

"That's not even most of it."

"Wow."

"Yeah. We may or may not see the taphofae today. Dartanya is a special case."

"I don't know if I could handle too many greetings like Dartanya's."

"I don't think anyone could quite greet you like Dartanya did. Alright, enough talking about cemeteries, let's go see them."

They portaled to the Poydras station and waited for the streetcar. Fay paid for both of their fares and they took a seat in the front, Fay pointing out buildings and houses as they went. They started at Greenwood with its giant society tombs, and rows and rows of above ground family tombs.

"They're like little houses." Jane marveled.

"Only much smaller with a ton more people inside."

Jane gave her a quizzical look.

"See all those names on the closure tablets?"

Jane nodded.

"Think pizza ovens." Fay said with a sardonic grin. "A person is put in the crypt, and they are left to bake through our delightfully soul crushingly hot summers and after a year and day the ashes and bits are pushed off the shelf down into the caveau to mingle with all the other ancestral bones. The year and a day thing, it's a witchy period of time, isn't it?"

"It is. One of many things borrowed from witches." she said with a hint of annoyance.

Fay smiled, "Let's meander to Oddfellow's, we will probably see the taphofae there, not only because he will sense our arrival but because he hangs out in the stone flower vase attached to the grave I want to show you. His name is Duckie and he himself is an odd fellow. So, this plot is a little different as the person is actually buried in the ground."

"An in-ground burial? How does that work?"

"They use what are called coping walls. The walls are built into the ground out of granite or marble and built up to three feet above the ground. Then it's filled in with dirt and gravel, protecting the area."

"Interesting, let's go."

They portaled straight into Oddfellow's and were immediately met by Duckie flying up with a flourish out of a stone vase. "Hellllllo, Faaaay. Oooh and who is this lovely creature?" He cooed with dramatic gestures as he circled Jane.

"Hey, Duckie. This is Jane. How did you know it was me?"

"Well hellllo Jane!" He said waggling his eyebrows. Then he turned in the air to face Fay and rolled his eyes with as much drama as he could muster, "of course it's you. You are my most frequent visitor and you always land in front of this grave because it's also your favorite."

"What's so special about this grave?" Jane asked.

Without a word both Fay and Duckie pointed down to the name engraved in the coping wall, it read *Funk*. Duckie started laughing at the look Jane was giving them and began flying around singing poorly but dramatically, *play that funky music dead boy.*

Jane rolled her eyes and stared incredulously at Fay and Duckie."The whole reason we are here is because this guy's name was FUNK?"

"Well yeah, and to say hi to Duckie, I mean look at how fantastic he is. Do we need more of a reason?"

"I guess not. Silly me, I was expecting something more profound."

"I haven't found a profound grave yet." She said, using air quotes. "I have found a petty and a power." Jane just stared at her so she continued blathering, "Sometimes I like to sneak in here with fresh flowers and put them in all the vases or lay them in front to the tombs, just to fuck with people since no one is supposed to be here. We can do that one day if you want."

"That actually sounds like it would be fun." Jane smiled despite herself, "Where else are we going?"

"Holt."

"Oh." Duckie said. "Fair warning. Des has been sulky."

"Thanks for the heads up." Fay said with a sigh. They walked the couple of blocks over to Holt chatting on the way.

"Who's Des?"

"Des Ta Toot, is the taphofae of Holt. He's always a bit

skittish and sullen. If it's bad enough that Duckie has made note of it, he must be grumpier than normal."

As they approached the cemetery a dog came running through the gates. Jane and Fay both turned and watched it, "Well, that was unusual, but not all that surprising." Fay muttered.

As they walked into the cemetery Jane's breath caught.

"Yeah, it has that effect on people."

"Everyone is buried in the ground here?"

"Yes."

"And there aren't coping walls?"

"No, not really."

"What happens when it rains?"

"Things surface."

They walked silently down the path taking in the scene. It was difficult for Jane, never having seen anything quite like it. Fay could see the overwhelmed look on her face. Without thinking she grabbed her hand and said, "Come on this is my favorite place to sit." Fay dragged Jane along to a giant oak tree, with waif-like tendrils of Spanish moss blowing in the slight breeze.

The trunk had more or less grown sideways so that you could walk

up it and perch, Fay led Jane up it to do just that. "Just sit a minute."

Fay said.

Jane nodded, tears brimming her eyes.

"Look for the beauty."

Jane nodded again, opened her mouth as if to speak and then shut

it again shaking her head slightly.

"This is why I say it's the most hauntingly beautiful and

sad."

"I understand that statement now." Jane said in a small

voice. She looked around again from their new vantage point at the

wooden cross markers and pieces of wood shaped like headstones

in varying colors with handwritten names and dates on them. Next

to those there were actual headstones, most of which were military

markers. Teddy bears and fake flowers strewn about in the uneven

high grass grounds. Piles of markers on top of each other, wood, and

granite alike. "Where do those markers belong?" Jane asked.

"No one is really sure. Those still living know where

their loved one went in the ground, but no one is for sure. The ground here floods and shifts a lot."

"That is heartbreaking."

"I mean yeah, it can be. And it's easy to focus on that, but the dead don't care where they're buried, they're dead. I think this cemetery is full of love. Families that cannot afford a granite marker make their own. They pour all of their love and grief into painting their loved one's name, date of birth and date of death on them. Actually, if you look closely a lot of them say sunrise and sunset for their birth and death date. I find that whole process terribly beautiful and meaningful. It's a proper way to get your hands dirty and truly delve into your grief instead of letting some unknown person engrave a name on a headstone or closure tablet."

"You really have such a unique outlook." Jane said almost in awe.

"Hello! Birthed from death and lived in this city my entire life. You tend to see every walk of life. This cemetery speaks more to New Orleans life than the others in some ways, it's poor, haunted, beautiful, and a little dirty, it speaks to the true nature of life and death."

"Yeah, I can kinda see that now. Seeing it through your eyes is definitely different from the overwhelming first look I was getting." Jane said.

"Now that you have a different perspective do you want to take a closer look or is this too much? If it's too much it's ok, I should have warned you a little more thoroughly than hauntingly beautiful and sad. A lot of people would say that about a normal cemetery."

"Hey, it's ok. I'm ok. Let's continue. I want to see it how you see it."

"If you're sure, then let's get out of this tree. Do you want to see the old crematorium in the back? I must warn you that Des lives in there."

"Sure." Jane said tentatively.

They continued to walk through the cemetery, Fay pointing out unique items, statues, flowers, rosary beads, handwritten notes, and the essence of love left behind. Trying to gauge Jane's comfort level as they went. They walked up to the crematorium and Fay called out.

"Des, you home?"

"Who's there? Leave me alone. Find somewhere else for these stupid orb things. Go awa… Oh! Fay. Hello." A small scraggly voice said.

"What's wrong, Des? Can I help?"

"No! Nothing. Can't talk about it. No. No. No. I must go!" the dingy shaggy haired taphofae turned and flew back into the crematorium and fell silent.

Fay noticed the goosebumps on her own arms. She ignored them and said, "Well, that was weird even for him. Shall we go?"

As the girls disappeared through the portal Des zipped back out, squeaked, and zipped back into his home as a dark shadow engulfed the entire crematorium.

March 11

Quickly scratching out some things while Jane is in the shower...

I may have fucked up with Holt.

Jane was so overwhelmed.

I feel so stupid taking her there without properly warning her.

I forget how overwhelming it can be to sensitives especially those that have never seen it before.

There's something up with Des, he's acting weirder than usual.

He kept rambling and he seemed frightened by something.

I'm not sure but I think I saw a shadow fall upon the crematorium as my portal closed. Maybe it was just light interference.

I think I have to go back to Holt without Jane tonight. If the day time was too much the spirits will definitely be too much especially if something is wonky.

Maybe tomorrow we will just lounge.

I'm going with Jane to Austin tomorrow evening. She has incoming souls and bodies.

I found myself sad that she was leaving so soon. I don't know what that's about, but I've already kinda got used to her being around only after a couple of days. I was so relieved when she invited me along I almost made a complete fool out of myself.

Me make a fool out of myself? SHOCKING, I know! Just tryin' to live up to my birthday.

It was really weird to wake up to someone in my bed this morning. It was even weirder when I realized she was in some kind of trance. I felt like an intruder in my own bed. She wanted me to stay though. I've never seen someone get a "download from the universe" as she referred to it. Since she has incoming animals that need death care, I will get to see her process and I am definitely intrigued after what I witnessed this morning.

-FF

Fay sat curled up in the oversized chair in the living room, lost in thought with a notebook in her lap when Jane emerged from the shower wearing a black T-shirt with a girl and a black cat on it and red and black polka dot pajama bottoms.

"Hey." She said quietly. "You ok?"

Fay blinked a couple times and looked at her. "Is that an Emily the Strange shirt?" She asked confusedly.

Jane laughed and sat down on the couch, "Yes, I've always had a thing for her. I knew pretty early on that I was not a normal child. You know the moniker for a Jane, is generally plain, and I've never been that. I have always been more of a strange Jane. Now answer my question, are you ok?"

"I see there will be no subject changes. Yeah, I think I need to go back to Holt. Something was weird. Des seemed out of sorts. He's always a little squirrelly, but not like this. He seemed…"

"Scared." Jane finished.

"Yeah. Having just met him I didn't think you would know to notice."

"There's being squirrelly and then there's being

scared. His whole being oozed fear except for one brief second when he saw it was you and then fear again."

"Ok, so I'm not crazy. I'm gonna take my team and go check it out. Will you be ok here with Ebs and Merla? I've already asked Bran to come back for an assist. I figure eyes in the air wouldn't be a bad idea."

"I can come with you." Jane began.

"No. You had a hard enough time today and it gets really rowdy and active there at night. Not all bad, but a lot to take in."

"I will take your word for it."

The team portaled to the end of the streetcar line and walked to Holt from there. They opted not to portal straight there because a portal would give them away immediately if there was trouble. They could hear the going's on at Holt well before they got to the gate. It always sounded like a raucous party at night. You could hear jazz and laughter and yelling and gunshots. This cemetery truly came alive at night. Bran took off for the sky, while Fay, Heck, and Nubs walked through the ghosts asking if any of the spirits had seen Des. The only answer they got was, "shadows". That's all the spirits would say.

They walked up to the crematorium and Heck hissed, "Don't touch it, it's hot."

"Hot," Fay whispered. "What do you mean hot?"

"Yeah, as if someone has at the very least tried to use it for what it is."

"What the fuck? Is that even possible?" Fay hissed.

"By normal means? No. By magical means? Yes. We need to get out of here. Des is either on the run or..." Heck trailed off looking at the crematorium. "Let's go." She finished.

Just then Bran swooped down and landed on Nubs' head so he could look Fay in the eye. Nubs grumbled in irritation at being a perch. "We need to go." Bran said just shy of being a frantic whisper. "All the cemetery crows are in a tizzy saying there is a shadow that moves through the cemetery. I don't know what it means but it makes me uncomfortable."

And with that they portaled home.

The portal opened and deposited the team in the living room. Jane looked up slightly startled as she sat in the oversized chair with Ebs in her lap and Merla perched on the mantel.

Fay sank into the couch, looking defeated. Bran perched next to Merla. Nubs and Heck sat on the couch with Fay. They relayed the weirdness of what they had experienced.

Fay sighed and said, "With whatever is going on here I think I should stay and see if we can figure out what happened to Des."

"Ok." Jane said sadly, but she understood.

"I think that's a horrible idea." Bran croaked at Fay. "We don't know for sure what, if anything, is going on. We all know that the line between this realm and that of the Otherside is very thin and blurry not only in this city, but especially at Holt. Things slip in and out all the time. Maybe something just spooked Des and he's hiding. If something nefarious is afoot and the shadow is something, it's possible it knows you were there today and poking around tonight. I think staying would be the worst idea. Whatever it is will either continue to hide from you or try to dispose of you like it may have done with Des. I think the best plan is for the two of you to get out of here for a few days."

"Seriously?" Fay asked incredulously.

"Yes." Heck hissed. "We will seek out the taphofae and keep a lookout for Des. We can skulk around Holt relatively unnoticed. Except for maybe Nubs. Claire can keep an eye on y'all in Austin and reach us if something happens."

"I am not a teenager, I can in fact take care of myself, goddammit." Fay argued.

"No one is saying that you can't." Heck hissed impatiently.

"Hey." Jane said, touching Fay's arm. Fay had been so flustered she hadn't noticed Jane's approach. As she looked up everything around them blurred in a green glow and then they were sitting alone on a completely different couch in a completely different house.

"Is this? Are we? Is this your house?"

"Yes, you looked like you were feeling cornered, so I made a decision. I figured we would end up here anyway."

Fay wanted to be mad, but she wasn't. She was relieved. "Thanks." She said quietly.

"You're not mad?"

"No. Just drained."

"Well, I'm sure I have some pjs that will fit you. My bathroom isn't quite the spectacle yours is, the tub is nice though. Come on." Jane led Fay upstairs to her small but quaint bathroom. The tub was a little longer than a standard tub and the back was slanted. Jane started the water and poured some Epsom salt and lavender oil in the bath. "Here's a towel and let me go grab some pajamas." Jane said exiting the bathroom and coming right back with a gray T-shirt and blue plaid pants.

Fay eyed her and the clothes suspiciously. She opened the shirt which read, *HOGWARTS*. She looked at Jane with a serious expression on her face. "Why the blue pants?"

Jane gave her a look and said, "Are you not a Ravenclaw?" Jane turned around and walked out, closing the door.

Fay smiled at the closed door then put the clothes down on the counter and slipped into the bath relaxing almost immediately. Maybe relaxing too much. The next thing Fay knew there was a quiet knock at the door. She then realized she had fallen asleep, and her bath water was cold.

"Fay? You ok in there?"

"Yeah, give me a sec." Fay answered groggily. She pulled the drain plug and slowly got out of the tub, dried off, and put her borrowed pajamas on. She slowly opened the door and saw Jane appear from the room next to the bathroom.

"Hey, you ok?" Jane asked, looking worried.

"Yeah, apparently a bath is exactly what I needed because I fell asleep."

"Yeah, I thought you might have, it's been over an hour and I was beginning to worry."

"Fuck, I'm sorry."

"Don't be, it's been quite the day. I do have a guest

room if you'd like to be alone."

"I don't." Fay said finally looking in Jane's eyes.

Jane met her gaze and said, "That's understandable. My room is right here, come on." Fay followed not really seeing her surroundings and collapsed into bed. Jane slowly laid down beside her and turned out the light. They both fell asleep.

The Twelfth of March

Jane woke up to Fay's flailing in the bed next to her. Sleepiness rapidly departed and she was wholly awake. She glanced at the clock and it was just after three in the morning. "Holy shit." Jane whispered. It looked like Fay was fighting for her life. She gently touched Fay's shoulder and nudged her to see if she would wake. She didn't, instead she turned and swung at her. Jane grabbed that wrist and moved it back to Fay's chest and laid down behind her grabbing her other arm and holding it to her own chest. She kept whispering, "You are ok, you are safe", she continued the mantra in her sleep.

As the sun rose Fay woke, first not realizing where she was. Then remembering. This was followed by the realization that she was restrained, followed by panic, followed by the knowledge that she was ok and safe, which she thought of all the thoughts she was having that was the most unlikely, followed by embarrassment as she realized what must have happened. She shuddered, she had dreamed that a shadow had come for her and her wings. She had also dreamt that Des wanted her wings because he didn't have his anymore.

"Fuck." She muttered into the pillow.

"Hey. It's ok." Jane said sleepily, loosening her death grip on Fay.

"No it's not. I lost my shit in my sleep, didn't I?"

"Yeah, kinda. You started flailing about. I tried to wake you, which didn't go well. So, I pinned your arms to you and kept repeating the mantra: you're ok, you're safe, over and over."

"Well, that explains that thought in my head I didn't recognize." Fay sat up and put her head in her hands. "I'm really sorry."

"Don't be, I'd rather you not wrestle whatever demon that was alone. Can I ask what that was all about?"

"My wings. Someone was trying to take them from me, a shadow creature, a dog maybe." She scrunched up her face trying to remember.

Jane reached like she was going to touch Fay's back and then thought better of it. "You don't talk about them often." She said instead.

"No, I don't." Fay shut down the topic.

"I'm sorry."

"I mean, I have been secretly blaming you this whole time." Fay said with a slight smile.

"Shut up!" Jane said getting out of bed disappearing down the hallway.

Fay slowly stood up and began to look around. She realized then that she hadn't seen a thing when she got here yesterday. The first thing she noticed was that the room was small. It felt cozy rather than small . It wasn't quite rectangular or quite round, but somewhere in between. There was a nook of three large arched windows with a built-in seat, black curtains mostly drawn. She was pulled to the window and when she opened the curtains fully, light blazed into the room, she looked out realizing they were on the second floor. After taking in the pristinely kept lawns she turned back to the room she was standing in. The bed they had been sleeping in was an ebony stained, ornately carved, wooden canopy, with all the curtains tied to the posters. She couldn't quite make out the carvings, but the curtains themselves appeared to be black satin with a black and silver gauzy flowery material sewn onto the satin. There were two nightstands and an armoire that matched the bed. There was nothing else in the room. The floors were old and creaky hardwoods that she suspected ran through the whole house, and the ceiling was painted like a galaxy. Fay was still staring at the ceiling when Jane came back in with two large cups of coffee.

"Hey." Jane said

"Hey. Is that coffee?" Fay asked, eyes brightening a fraction.

"Yeah." Jane said, "let's sit." She gestured with her head as she walked over to the window seat with both cups of coffee.

Fay turned and followed. She sat down across from Jane and gratefully took the coffee from her. They both stared out the window for a minute. Fay really focused and realized the lawn was actually detailed landscaping with rose bushes, irises, oak trees, willow trees, statues of animals, benches, mausoleum like buildings, and what looked to be grave markers. Jane was watching her, and she could sense it. She looked closer to the house and noticed there was a 1980's Cadillac hearse parked with one side facing the house and one facing the drive. The paint job consisted of animals and rainbows with McMortem's Rainbow Pet Cemetery, painted across the door panels, she assumed on both sides. She looked at Jane then.

"This is quite impressive, now that I'm really seeing it."

"We can walk the grounds later if you want."

"I would like that. I had no idea we were on the second floor until about five minutes ago, but I vaguely recall walking up some stairs last night. What was this room originally supposed to be? It seems too small to have been a bedroom."

"You were pretty out of it last night and this was just a sitting room; the master is down the hall past the bathroom along with two other bedrooms and a small kitchen. I however like to cocoon when I sleep, so I took the smallest room and put a canopy bed in here so I can close it off even more if I want. This window situation keeps it from feeling claustrophobic, I think." She said, gesturing at the area in which they were sitting. "I didn't close the canopy last night because I didn't want you to wake up and be completely confused or feel trapped."

"Appreciated. What do you do with all the other rooms?"

"So, this place was an abandoned funeral home, sitting on five acres. It was already set up for what I needed. The first floor is my business set up which I can show you later. This floor was and is the living quarters. Claire and Ebs sleep in the master. One of the rooms with similar windows to this room is my library and office. The other room is kinda just storage and pantry items. The attic is where all my witchy stuff is. We will be spending a lot of time up there tonight."

"Wow." Was all Fay could say. "And the hearse?" She followed up.

"Came with the house. I had a local artist paint it as a billboard for my company. I drive it occasionally."

"That's fucking cool!"

"Glad you approve." Jane laughed.

Fay's eyes grew serious, the weariness creeping back into her features, "Have you heard from anyone yet this morning?"

Jane's smile faded, "I have. They said that they haven't seen or heard anything out of the ordinary other than Des's house. They are going to check in with the other taphofae and reach out again later. Also, Heck is supposed to be sending you a bag with clothes and personal items."

Just then a gold glow emanated from the hallway followed by a loud thump and the padding of small feet. Fay rolled her eyes as the black cat sauntered in.

"Hey Heck."

"Hey. Before you ask, the news is that there isn't any. We've already talked to most of the taphofae, and they haven't seen any out of the ordinary weird stuff, just the normal weird stuff that happens in our city. They also say that it's been a while, but Des has disappeared before more than once. They also don't put it past him to set his own home to burn when he left, if he was in a paranoid state."

Fay eyed her. "Ok."

"Look Fay, you know us, we will keep patrolling, but everything looks all clear. I'm not saying that you didn't see or feel something. The change of the city's energy alone could have triggered something for him. He's been here forever, and he never left his post before Katrina, but as soon as the bodies settled, he did disappear for a while. "

"That makes sense. Just keep an eye out for him, please."

"Of course. Your bag is in the hall." Heck studied her, "Try to enjoy yourself. And Fay, keep your demons where they belong, in hell."

"There isn't a hell."

"Isn't there, halfling?" Heck said, turning back the way she came.

"Oh hey," Fay said, changing the subject. "Did you pack my notebook?"

"You wound me." The cat said as she disappeared in a golden glow.

"Didn't think one could wound a goddess." She grumbled sarcastically as she walked over and picked her bag up. She looked inside there on top was her notebook and with a typed note:

Not bad for no thumbs.

-H

Fay turned around to show Jane the note, but realized she was gawking at her. "What?" She said immediately defensive.

"Are those sunflowers all over your bag?"

"What?" Fay said, looking down. "Fuck you! I like sunflowers."

"Ok... Ok ..." Jane laughed, "just a little surprising is all."

"Well, it's good to know I can surprise you."

"You have no idea." Jane mumbled into her coffee cup.

Jane finished her coffee and went to shower and get dressed. Fay grabbed her notebook and headed back to the window seat.

March 12

Things are weird. I went back to Holt with the team. The spirits were acting weird. So were the crows. They kept talking about shadows. When I went to check on Des, he was gone. The no longer viable crematorium was hot when we arrived. HOT! Like in use!

Apparently he has a history of disappearing and the others wouldn't put it past him to set his own home to burn.

I don't know, I swore I saw a shadow or something as we portaled out of there earlier in the day.

The team wanted Jane and me to leave a day early and to lay low in case we were seen either time.

In case I'm right, and it's not just a flighty faery!

Something feels off, I just don't know what.

I felt cornered by the team and like they felt I was overreacting, and Jane... just knew. She portaled us straight to her house last night. I wanted to be pissed, but I found myself more relieved than anything.

I was so fucking out of it that I fell asleep in her tub and really have no idea what the rest of the house looks like other than her cocoon of a bedroom.

It's different, but I like it.

The dreams are back. Fuck.

No human other than Marie has witnessed the insanity of the nightmares, until last night that is. Nothing good happens when the dreams come...

I woke up this morning with Jane spooning me. And I had no idea how much I wanted that. Then I realized she was restraining me. My arms were pinned to my own body. The dreams came flooding back and I realized she was holding me to keep me and her safe... from me.

That realization cut through my heart and soul like a scythe. It wasn't want, it was necessity.

I was so embarrassed. I'm still embarrassed.

I almost told her about the dreams, about how they haunt me, about how painful the invisible weight tethered to my back is, about how afraid I am of losing something I don't really even have.

It seems that statement could be true about more than just my wings.

Pull yourself together Fay.

-FF

Fay put her notebook away and pulled out a pair of faded jeans and a t-shirt with a strangely illustrated bat on it. She grabbed her bra and underwear and quickly changed. She attempted to brush her hair and gave up, pulling it into a messy bun. Wishing she hadn't fallen asleep in the tub leaving her hair to fend for itself. Now they were at war with each other. As she started to follow the thoughts of waging war with her hair with tiny little helmets and swords. There was a light knock at the door.

"Come in." Fay said.

Jane walked in and stared at Fay's shirt. "Are you psychic?"

"Considering I didn't see that question coming, I'm gonna go with no. Why?"

"Well, I was thinking we could go watch the bats at sunset under Congress Bridge. We can take the hearse downtown if you want, and then veil ourselves to get close. They've closed it down because of the crowds, but if they can't see us, they can't stop us." Jane winked.

"That sounds awesome."

"Cool, are you ready for the grand tour?"

"Sure." Fay got up and followed Jane into the hall.

"This is the bathroom, but after last night I could see where you would mistake it for a bedroom." Fay blushed embarrassed. "Stop that, I'm teasing you." Jane flipped on the light. "Like I said last night, not as dramatic as yours, but the lavender purple and dark gray are calming to me."

"Me too, apparently." Fay smiled slightly.

Jane smiled back, "Come on. Over here is Claire and Ebs' room."

Fay peered in and almost burst out laughing but thought it to be rude. She bit down on her lip and whispered, "I'm sorry, but are those bunk beds with a slide?" Her eyes began to water, then she took a deep breath, turned back to the room and said, "Hey Claire."

Claire was sprawled out on the bottom bunk watching what sounded like a crime documentary. "Oh, hey Fay." She said with a deer houndish smile. Then she went back to watching TV.

They continued walking and Fay said, "I have so many

questions, but first is why the slide?"

"Oh. My. Gods. Ebs demanded it! I'm so glad I got it for him because it tickles me to see him sprawled out splay legged and oh so undignified going down that thing. He runs up it too and every so often he doesn't get enough speed and ends up sliding down. And he would kill me if he knew I told you! And I believe he could too with how many crime shows he's been subjected to because of the junkie in there."

"Oh man! I need to see that!" Fay exclaimed. "And your impending murder brings me to question two, crime documentaries?"

"Dude. I'm pretty sure Claire was human in a former life, but she won't say. What else?"

"I think that's all I have for now. My brain has a lot to process with those two answers."

"Ok, well, here's the small kitchen, it's about a third of the size of the kitchen downstairs. Across the hall here is the library and sitting room. Jane opened the door and Fay could see several cases with books stacked and strewn this way and that.

"Well, that's definitely an interesting organizational style."

"Shut up. It works for me."

"Sure, so are they strewn about alphabetically and piled by genre?" Fay continued.

"Shut up. This room is mostly storage. Let's go downstairs." she said passing the final room heading back toward the stairs.

"Do you store other things like you store your books?"

"Shut up."

"Wait, I thought you said you had a guest room?"

"Yeah, there's a bed in there somewhere."

"Now I know it's as bad as the library. You don't know where the bed is?"

"Shut up, Fay." Jane called as she walked down the creaky stairs. Fay grinned and followed.

They seemingly appeared in the front room of the house, as the staircase was completely hidden by a wall. As they hit the last step Jane said, "So, this is the parlor where I meet with people and where we portaled into last night. Some people actually pre-plan for their pet's death before their own. Others are blindsided. I have brochures with pricing for basic cremation, burial plots, caskets, urns, and more. Some people want actual ceremonies. I also subcontract out for people who want articulated skeletons or taxidermy. They get their own display area. I love it, but it really weirds some people out."

"What made you decide to add those services, especially if it cost you business?"

"It's not about that. Our boss sees to it that we are taken care of , as you know. So I don't have to worry about the bottom line as much, I can afford to help people, it's about getting people the closure they need. I make sure I have enough money to look like a real business and to pay my apprentice. I only call her that because I am training her to take over, we're actually quite good friends. Since, eventually, people will notice that we death workers don't age at the same rate as normal humans, I'm gonna have to sit in the shadows for a few decades. Anyway, several years ago I had a customer call and ask if it would be possible to have her cat buried so it would have a safe place to decompose then she wanted to dig it up for the bones. I didn't have a good answer for her, luckily her cat wasn't close to dying. She was doing research to see if what she wanted was possible. So I started researching. I had taken a taxidermy class a year or two before and became friends with the chick who runs it. She said that her and her partner are both skilled in taxidermy and skeleton articulation. So they pay a small fee to have a display here and I get a small percentage of the money they make from someone I refer to them. Sometimes they hold classes here which is fun." She said as they walked through the display room of varying sizes of casket and urns, unlocking the door at the back of the room.

Fay followed her in, "Whoa, these are badass." In the smaller room there stood a cat skeleton, a dog skeleton, and a rabbit. On the other side of the room stood a taxidermy German Shepard, rat, cat, and parakeet. "Damn. These are awesome."

"Yes, I think they're worth offering to my clients."

They walked back through toward the back of the house. "Here we have what would normally be a dining room, but we use it as a celebration of life/ funeral/ classroom. Then through here is the kitchen which is more or less used for storing bodies when necessary and baking paw prints rather than cookies. There's a restroom to the right. Out here is the garage which is where I receive the animals. That's pretty much the interior. Let's head out to the grounds."

They walked back through the house out the front door and towards the manicured lawns. Fay looked around in wonder at the incredible lawns and tiny headstones. There were statues of all sorts of animals. Dogs and cats, of course, but also bearded dragons, ferrets, goldfish, and turtles. There were marble dog houses and cat trees.

"Is that a mausoleum?" Fay said pointing.

"Yes, kinda. It's a family plot of sorts. There is a couple that came to me a few years ago and asked to build this." They veered that way. "It's for ashes. They have placed the ashes of their animals here that have already crossed. With the glass faced cubbies people can see the photo, paw print, and urn if they wish to come in and take a look. And people come and look. I'm pretty sure my place is listed on Atlas Obscura. Anyways, their will states that

when they pass their ashes are to be given to me to be placed in the

larger cubby over there, so they can rest easy with all their animals."

The interior of the mausoleum was three walls of glass faced

cubbies There were currently ten spots filled with two birds, a

rabbit, a goldfish, 3 cats and 4 dogs. All having framed pictures and

those with paws had prints. There was room for at least forty more

animals plus room for the human urns.

"How many animals do they expect to have?" Fay said,

looking around.

"Well, they currently have nine including the birds.

They have also made it clear that if I get rescue or strays that come

into my care once they have passed that I can fill in the extra spots

as I see fit. They're pretty cool people."

"They sound like it. Are those also mausoleums?

People really seem to care about their animals here."

"So these are kinda like your society tombs in New

Orleans. This one is the final resting place for the familiars of

witches. Hence "Familiars" carved above the entrance. The one over there was donated for rescues to be placed in." They walked into the Familiars building and Jane continued, " a witch's bond to their familiar is almost as strong as the bond we have with our cats. Many in the cemetery are familiars, this is for those that can't afford a plot, but want to honor their companion. I will always find a way to help a fellow witch honor their dead, animal or otherwise. I feel like power resonates in this place more than the others."

"I never really thought about all that. Not being a witch myself and the only witch I know also happens to be a banshee. I'm glad you have this space and understanding for them."

"Me too. Katrina is what really did it for me. All those animals, just tossed aside. It still hurts my soul. To this day I will not do communal cremations, not even if the city asks for my assistance with their unadoptables. I cry for them the most."

"Speaking of that. Where's the crematorium?"

"Further out back. I don't like people to see it."

"That's fair."

They continued walking in companionable silence through the grounds before returning to the house to rest a bit.

"I'm gonna try to nap before we head out to see the bats. Tonight will be very draining for me."

"Ok, we don't have to go see the bats tonight."

"No, that's not the issue, seeing the bats fly out boosts my energy. Neither of us slept very well last night I imagine. So I'm gonna lay down. You're more than welcome to join me."

"Gods, I am so sorry about that." Fay sighed, intrusive thoughts seeping in.

"Stop it. I've already told you." Jane took a step toward her, but Fay stepped back. "Ok." Jane said slowly, feeling Fay shutdown. "I'm gonna go lay down. If you want to lay down in another room, you can go lay down in the bed with Claire or you can brave the guest room." Jane said slowly moving away and up the stairs.

"Goddamnit" Fay grumbled, as she stood there in her own misery for a few minutes before ascending the antique stairs herself. She walked past Jane's room, the door was open but the bed curtains were drawn. She truly didn't wish to bother her, so she went to Claire's room. "Hey pooch."

Claire raised her head and smiled "You are so disrespectful." she said with no conviction. "Come to watch this thrilling crime documentary with me?"

"Obviously." Fay smiled and curled up in the bed laying her head on Claire's boney curly haired hip, and promptly fell asleep to the droning monotone voice of the narrator.

When Jane awoke from her nap. She found herself a little disappointed to be in her bed alone. She sat up and turned, letting her legs dangle off the bed a minute. Then she stood up and slowly made her way over to Claire's room. Her heart softened and her eyes welled a little. Fay looked so peaceful and childlike curled up, head on Claire's hip, her fingers tangled in Claire's fur. Jane crept in the room. Claire raised her head and looked at her. "Thank you." Jane whispered

Claire sighed heavily, "She didn't watch one second of the documentary." And she put her head back down on the bed.

Jane chuckled at that and whispered. "You're such a

true crime snob." She sat gently down on the bed not wanting to startle Fay, and placed her hand on her shoulder and said, "Fay?"

Fay opened one groggy eye and said, "I totally watched at least one second of the documentary." And she smiled.

Claire chuffed in annoyance and Jane burst out laughing at the two of them.

Fay smiled, "is it time to go?"

"I figured we could freshen up and then the three of us could get some food to go from Texas Chili Parlor and eat while we watch the bats."

"That sounds great." Fay said and unfolded herself following Jane down the hall to retrieve her bag from Jane's room. She grabbed her toothbrush and hairbrush and headed for the bathroom. Jane was already in there but waved her in. Fay set her brush on the counter and started brushing her teeth, glaring at the knot of hair on her head.

Jane noticed and said, "What's that face about?"

Fay pointed and glared at the mess of her hair, spit and said, "If I had been in my right mind I never would have gone to sleep with wet hair." She jammed her toothbrush back in her mouth annoyed.

"I have a trick to fix it if you'll let me."

Fay cocked an eyebrow suspiciously, but made a gesture of "carry on" with her hands.

Jane very gently undid the mess of blond tangled hair on Fay's head letting it fall. She whispered,   "Untangle at the root, untangle at the ends, let this hair hang smooth again." As she ran her fingers through Fay's hair.

Fay had goosebumps running down her body that she was trying to ignore. She spit out her toothpaste and looked at her perfect hair and said into the mirror, "You cheated!"

Jane responded, "I told you before I'm good with hair. Are you complaining? Because I can reverse the spell."

"No, no, no need for that." Fay said followed by,"I see witchcraft has its advantages."

Jane just smiled as she left the bathroom.

When the two women came downstairs Claire was waiting by the door looking regal. Fay looked at her and snarked,

"I'm surprised you could be pulled away from your crime shows."

"There's a lot I would do for a burger and fries from TCP."

"I don't even want to know." Fay said, scrunching up her face.

"Ok, you two, are y'all ready?" Jane asked.

They piled into the colorful hearse and headed for downtown Austin. It was about a 20 mile drive, but Fay didn't mind. She enjoyed watching the people look at the car. If only they really knew that the car was carrying three harbingers of death, one a witch and one a halfling. She found herself so amused that she looked at Jane and said, "You live in a city with the motto "Keep Austin Weird", and still they think you're weird here, don't they?"

Jane just deadpanned back, "I prefer Strange." They parked a couple blocks from the Congress Street bridge. Jane got out of the car and placed business cards on the windshield and windows. Fay stared at her. "Hey, people stop, and I guarantee all the cards will be gone when we get back. So it's roughly a 30 minute walk to TCP. I figured we could walk there and portal to a spot near the bridge. I'm gonna call the order in, I figured three cheese burgers with fries and a side of chili, and a 6 pack of mixed ciders because apparently that's a thing now."

"Oh yeah, I forgot this isn't New Orleans where we can actively walk around with alcohol."

"No, this alcohol to-go thing is definitely new to the pandemic."

They walked as Jane pointed out different things. She mused about the pink color of the capitol building in such a "masculine" state. She talked about how crazy it gets during college football season. When they walked in to get their order Fay looked around and said quietly to Jane, "Wasn't this in a Tarantino flick?"

"Yeah, but they don't like to talk about it." Jane scoffed.

"I don't care, this is awesome. I love that movie!"

"Glad I could accommodate." Jane said as she grabbed their stuff from the bar handing Fay the ciders. As they rounded the corner, Claire on their heels, they disappeared.

They walked out of Jane's portal on to the banks of Lady Bird Lake, right under a lovely tree. They made sure to keep veils in place as they sat down to devour their dinner.

Fay was awed by the bats. Sitting in that place with Jane watching the bats fly frantically from under the bridge blanketing the sky with tiny black stars brought her more joy than she knew what to do with. So she tamped that shit right back down where it belonged. She didn't realize Jane was watching whatever inner struggle was going on.

"Cool, huh?" Jane asked, trying to stop whatever Fay was overthinking.

"It was fantastic." Fay beamed at her.

"This is nothing, wait til peak season in about August when over twice as many fly out."

"Really? I'm so there, or here rather."

Jane laughed, "We better get back. Still got a long night ahead of us."

"So what does tonight entail?"

"A bunch of woo woo witchy shit." Jane grinned.

"Well the little bit of your woo woo witchy shit that

I've experienced has impressed me. Lead the way."

They walked back to the car and sure enough all the business cards were gone.

When they arrived at Jane's, she put the car in park and said, "I think I'm gonna make a cup of tea before I start, that always seems to help center me and we can start whenever you're ready."

"First off, tea sounds delightful, and two, we will start whenever you're ready. I'm not here to hold you back."

"Ok." Jane said, getting out of the car.

They walked inside and up the stairs to the small kitchen. Claire had gone back to her room and the slow calming cadence of the true crime narrator filtered through the house. Jane made each of them a cup of lavender lemon tea. Handed Fay hers and said, "Come on. Let's go up."

They made their way back toward Jane's room and toward the stairs, but instead of turning right to go downstairs, Jane made a seemingly impossible left turn and there hidden by another wall was a staircase leading to the attic. Jane went up the stairs first with Fay close behind. They stood there for a moment. Fay noticed one candle in a lantern by the window that appeared to have been burning for a very very long time. The white wax looked as if it melted upon itself over and over, yet staying neatly in the confines of the lantern, as soon as the wax touched the bottom it would disappear. Jane watched her and said, "It's enchanted. I keep it burning so that any soul that may find itself lost will see the light and come to me." She whispered."Spark!" And the whole room lit up with candlelight. She smiled at the look on Fay's face.

"Has anyone reached out to you because of the candle?" She said trying to take everything In.

"Yes actually. A couple times, but one in particular stands out. Usually if I interact with a soul it's after the body of the creature has come into my care, sometimes the soul moves on without a second glance. Others stay with their human until they cross. So, one day this scruffy black cat named Jack came to me after he crossed, but before crossing the bridge. He said many years ago his first mom was in a car wreck and he always traveled with her. It was night and when the door was opened, he ran out. He asked me to find her. Gave me her name, that they lived in Oklahoma at the time, but they were from the Dallas area. He told me to tell her, he's

sorry he ran from the car and caused her so much pain. He said, tell

her there was a little girl that needed him more. He had a good life

with the girl, but he never forgot her either."

Fay was trying to subtly wipe tears from her eyes and

asked," Did you find her?"

"Are you crying?" Jane asked, a touch surprised.

"What? No." Fay said a little too defensively.

"Sure." Jane said," And yes, I did find her. And him

actually. His new human had him interred here, she was 18 and

heartbroken and told me she had no idea why she was here, but

there at her feet was the spirit of Jack. So I told her what he had told

me. I didn't realize his body was coming because he came to me as

Jack, but my download was for Harry which was what his new mom

had named him. She said he reminded her of Harry Potter because

his fur was always a ruffled uneven mess. She had him cremated

and placed in one of the glass-faced cubbies in one of the

communal mausoleums. She gave me a photo of him and told me to

put Harry Jack: the cat that stole the heart of two women. She also told me if I found his previous human to tell her where he is and that she is more than welcome to place a photograph of Jack in there to go with the one of Harry. It wasn't easy but Kaila Knoll with Kaila being spelled with an "I" instead of a "y" made it easier. So I sent a letter on McMortem's letterhead. I pretty much started with, I know this sounds strange but... and then, I told her all that I knew. She wrote back with a letter for the other woman and two copies of pictures of Jack. One for his cubby and one for his other mom. They both came up here and met one day, and sat talking on one of the benches sharing photos and stories with Harry Jack laying on the bench between them. It was really fucking cool and well, magical." She finished with a smirk.

"It definitely is fucking cool and magical." Fay said in awe of the story and the attic. "So what am I looking at here?"

"So this table over here under the lantern, is my working altar. This is where we will be for the most of tonight." She said walking toward an arched window overlooking the front lawns. "Over here is where I store things, no jokes." she said pointing at Fay, and then walked down the long side wall lined with hutches. "

There are candles of every color in here, though most are black and white." She said opening a glass faced door with several boxes of tea lights, four inch to twelve inch tapers. "In here are various types of candle holders. Here are different types of incense , though mostly I use a scent called graveyard dirt, which I order from New Orleans actually. Down here in these library card holders I have several different copies of complete sets of tarot cards sorted by card type. So those are all one of cups, those are all three of swords, those are all death cards, I make about 10x as many death cards for obvious reasons. Over here are herbs, and here are stones and crystals. I mostly use rainbow obsidian and labradorite because they most remind me of the rainbow bridge. In this drawer are sachet bags of varying colors. These shelves are filled with little stone animal figurines, mostly cats and dogs, but others too. These drawers have fabric swatches. I like to bundle everything together before putting it in the bag. Over here on this back wall and window I have my offerings altar. I leave coins, candles, found objects, and anything else that feels right. Sometimes it's pictures, or alcohol."

"May I? " Fay asked.

"Of course." Jane said

Fay produced a crumpled pack of clove cigarettes out of one of her boots. She pulled one out and placed it carefully on the table."Living in New Orleans you learn at a very young age that entities are fond of liquor and tobacco, so I always carry something on me."

"Specifically Clove cigarettes?"

"Well no, but being a child of death, I figure I'm allowed a clove once in a while."

"Of course." Jane said. "So I've got five spell bags to make tonight. Here are the names I got on my download the other day." She said handing Fay a list:

Abby:Dog /15 /old age /cremated,

Sunshine: Dog/ 3 hit by a car /cremated

Moon:Cat /3 /unexpected health complications / familiar /burial with graveside ceremony

Lily:dog/15/old age/cremated 2 boxes shared ashes

Fatty: cat/23/over being alive/ cremated

Fay stared at the list and looked up and asked, "Over being alive is a cause of death?"

"Sometimes they are brutally honest. Twenty-three is really freaking old for a normal cat. It's easy to forget when our cats are meant to be with us as long as we live... I think."

"Yes it is easy to forget that not everyone knows the joys of somewhat immortal talking cats. And yes, I think they're meant to be with us for life. Marie's cat, Voodoo, has been with her since birth I believe, though I do believe he's had to jump bodies a few times." Fay said.

"So we will need five sachet bags, four pieces of rainbow obsidian, one piece of labradorite, five death tarot cards and one high priestess tarot, some graveyard dirt incense, three cat figurines and two dogs." Jane wandered around the room gathering all of her items. She laid out five bags along with five small pieces of black cloth with a white paw print pattern. In the fabric she placed either a cat or dog figure, a death card, the obsidian or labradorite, and sprinkled a little bit of graveyard dirt in each. In one of the cat ones she placed a high priestess card. She looked at Fay and said," this one is for a witch's familiar thus the high priestess card. I'm about to wrap these bundles up, spritz them with moon water, and let them sit here in the moonlight. I will ask Hecate to bless them and the souls they represent. Tomorrow I will make a tag for each and take them downstairs and they will be given to the animal's person. Sara will be in tomorrow and she can handle everything except the burial. I have handed a lot of the responsibilities over to her, but I am always present if it is a witch's familiar. I believe we will be burying Moon tomorrow evening. After that we can head back to your place."

"Okay." Fay agreed.

Jane finished up for the evening and they went back downstairs. They both headed for the window seat in Jane's room without saying a word. "After Sara gets here in the morning and I give her instructions, I will have most of the day off. I will need to be back by probably two in the afternoon to prepare Moon's body for burial. There is a cemetery I want to show you. The cemetery kinda spills out. It's really a visual thing."

"Sounds good." Fay yawned. "I'm pretty worn out despite the nap."

"Me too."

They both stood. Jane opened the wardrobe to retrieve her pajamas and Fay pulled a fresh set out of her bag. Fay finished first and climbed into the bed with her notebook in hand, but found herself too tired to write. She set it on the nightstand and laid down. Jane walked back in the room at that moment. "Hey, if you want to close the curtains, it's not a big deal, I know where I am now."

"Ok." Jane said with a smile and whispered, "cocoon." All of the curtains closed around them.

Fay shook her head, "Nice.", and then looked at Jane again realizing what shirts they were wearing, "You actually wear the Jane shirt I sent?'

"Why wouldn't I? I too loved that show growing up. Plus I believe the note that came along with it said something to the effect of, "Thanks for always being the Jane to my Daria." She pointed at the Daria shirt Fay was currently wearing. They both

blushed and smiled and Jane turned out the light.

132

The Thirteenth of March

When Fay woke up the next morning she immediately knew she was alone in the bed, but she could smell coffee. She peeked her head out of the curtain to find a hot cup of coffee on the nightstand with a note.

I didn't know how late you would sleep. I'm downstairs helping Sara get everything ready for the day. No matter what time you wake the coffee should be the perfect drinking temperature.

Life hack: keep a witch around.

-Jane

Fay reached over and grabbed the cup, took a big gulp of it, and was still surprised despite Jane's note, to find the coffee to be the perfect temperature. She shook her head smiling. She reached back out and took her notebook from the nightstand, as she turned back she saw the slightest movement.

"What the Heck!" Fay exclaimed.

"That's not very original, halfling." Heck chuckled.

"I hate you." Fay said, narrowing her eyes.

"No, you don't." The cat said flatly. "Do you want a report or not?"

"Of course, I do." Fay growled.

"There is literally nothing to report. The spirits at Holt have calmed down. I really think the line between here and the Otherside may have blurred, and everyone was in a tizzy. No sign of Des, but everyone says this is not that abnormal for him. Please try to enjoy yourself."

"Ok, thanks for the update. I think we are headed back either tonight or tomorrow morning."

"Ok. See you later." Hecate said and backed into her own portal.

March 13

So, things seem to be better. Heck just showed up and scared me half to death (being created half by death if I'm scared half to death does that make me wholly death? Cue existential crisis) Anyway she thinks she's funny, just appearing next to me when my back is turned. Bitch. She popped in (literally) to let me know that everything seems to be ok now. Still no Des but as everyone keeps telling me that's not that unusual. I don't know. I just feel like something's not right. Maybe it's just the city being closed down.

Yesterday was really cool. Seeing where Jane lives and works. Really seeing and experiencing Jane in her element, as a witch. I learned a lot. Many deep things but also that she can untangle my rats nest of hair and keep coffee at the perfect temperature. If I knew that this was part of it I would have petitioned for witchy abilities. (That is how you become a witch right? By petition)

We ate greasy bar food from Texas Chili Parlor, which was featured in a Tarantino flick. Apparently, they're over it, but I don't care. It was fucking awesome to be in there even if it was just for a minute. We sat under a tree by the lake and watched thousands upon thousands of tiny bats fly out from under a bridge. It was cool.

The only negative thing yesterday was me. I shut Jane out a couple times. I was so embarrassed for someone to see that. I don't know what exactly happens but I know what my bed looks like when I wake and Heck gives me vague details. She has a unique perspective of being able to see what is going on inside and outside of my head. Fuckin' peeper.

<u>Side note</u>: Jane's grim, Claire, is addicted to true crime documentaries, and despite being super bony makes a great pillow. She also drinks cider using her teeth to hold the bottle and tip it back. I'm so glad no one could see us. A PETA person would have lost their shit if they saw that. I can't help but laugh at the absurdity of that grim. She is the complete opposite of Nubs.

<u>Side note x2</u>: Jane wore the Jane Lane shirt I sent her. This is me not reading anything into it or examining why it makes me so happy that she does.

-FF

Fay set her notebook down and was finishing her coffee when she heard a whisper that sounded like, *butterfly*. As she was questioning what she heard the curtains began to open on their own. She looked around bewildered and saw Jane's smiling face.

"Did you whisper butterfly?" Fay asked quizzically.

"Yes." Jane laughed. "If the command cocoon closes them." She waved her hand slightly and the curtains were closing again. "It stands to reason," she continued, "That butterfly would open them." She finished with another slight wave of her hand, and the curtains opened again.

"Well yes I guess it is the only logical conclusion, OR the command could be moth."

"Sure, except when I think of moths, being who and what we are, I always see the Death's-head Hawk-moth from The Silence of the Lambs movie poster. So I would probably have to make the command, Hello Clarice."

Fay beamed, "That's a great idea! Oh, and thanks for the coffee." She said, raising the cup to her face.

"You're welcome." Jane said. "Sara is set up so I'm free to go whenever."

"Ok well, let me take a quick shower and I can be ready to go in about thirty minutes."

"Cool, no rush. The cats are coming. The cemetery I want to take you to has a no pets sign and they want their pictures taken."

Fay rolled her eyes, "Of course they do."

"I'm gonna go help Sara with paw prints then. It's like arts and crafts, but extreme."

"As in extremely dead." Fay dead panned.

"Well, yes." Jane smiled and disappeared down the stairs.

Fay turned and planted her feet on the wood floor and pushed herself up. Her wings felt heavy today despite everything being seemingly fine. She rummaged through her bag and found a shirt that said, *I'll burn that bridge when I get to it*. She grabbed that, a pair of black jeans, and underwear. She padded into the bathroom. Once properly bathed and dressed she made her way down the stairs and into the parlor.

"Hello?" She called.

"Back here."

"Hey." Fay said

"Hey." Jane said smiling, hands and smock covered in a white substance. She then looked down at her hands and said, "clean hands." All the particles of clay fell to the floor.

"I don't think that's a CDC approved method of hand washing." Fay said.

"She's showing off for you." Called a voice as a dark-haired woman appeared out of the garage.

"Shut. Up. Sara." Jane said with a glare.

"Is that so?" Fay asked with a devilish grin.

"I hate both of you." Jane said.

"No, you don't!" Fay and Sara said in unison.

They grinned at each other as Jane growled and walked out of the room.

Fay crossed the room, "Fay Finis."

"Sara Outlaw." Sara said, reaching to shake Fay's hand.

"Your last name is Outlaw? Like seriously?"

"That's what my birth certificate claims anyway."

"Please tell me you have guns on hip holsters that you can twirl!"

"You mean like these?" Sara asked, her hazel eyes sparkling almost like burning embers, as she drew back the lab coat she was wearing.

"No. Fucking. Way." Fay punctuated.

"Draw." Sara said and the guns undid themselves from their holsters. "Twirl" she said, and the guns spun as if on her finger. "Hands" and the guns fit into her hands.

"Now who's showing off?" Jane asked, leaning against the doorway.

Sara laughed and holstered her guns, "I mean, what is a girl to do with a name and gifts like mine? Of course, one of the first things I taught myself with and without magic was gun twirling. So yeah, maybe I'm showing off a little." And she winked at Jane.

"Come on Jane, that was pretty awesome. That's some real Texas shit right there!" Fay said "some witchy Texas outlaw shit at that."

Jane rolled her eyes, "Y'all meeting was a horrible idea. Hindsight and all that. Are you ready?"

"Yeah, I'm ready." Fay grinned.

Just then both teams minus the beetles appeared around them. "Ok let's go." Heck said.

"All of us?" Jane asked, arching an eyebrow.

"Yes, long enough for a couple group photos. Then the crows and grims will take their leave." Heck answered, turning to create a portal.

"That's the part I'm most looking forward to." Nubs muttered.

They walked through the portal and out into the gates of Oakwood Cemetery. Fay stared at the city ordinance signs posted. NO PETS ALLOWED IN CEMETERY with an outline of a dog and cat. The next sign said NO FIRES IN CEMETERY. Fay looked at Jane and cried, "What kind of lame ass cemetery did you bring me to? I came here to build fires with my pets." She said, gesturing at the menagerie and pulled out a zippo with an evil grin.

Jane burst out laughing, "I'm so sorry to disappoint. Let's get this picture taken." she said letting her phone hover in the air.

They took several pictures with various amounts of humans and animals. Once they finished, the cats took off to explore the grounds, the crows took to the trees, and the grims lumbered through portals to their respective dens.

"Ok." Jane said impatiently, "Now that photo time is done. Come check this out!"

They walked toward and out the gates. Fay immediately stopped, "What the fuck am I looking at?"

"No one knows. I told you it was weird." On the adjacent corner to the cemetery gates, barely stood an abandoned crack den of a house. The yard was full of engraved headstones.

"Those are people's headstones." Fay said drawn across the street to the house.

"That's what we thought. None of these people are

listed as buried here, or not in this cemetery, rather. They're all buried in Austin though. And they all have headstones exactly like these. Well. Except solid." Jane said as she reached her hand into and through a headstone that said, *Flowers*.

"It's not real?"

"No, not in a mortal sense. As far as I can tell only death workers and witches can see it."

"What… who?" Fay began. "Why?" She trailed off.

"All valid questions with no answers. Now that I've blown you away, let's take a leisurely walk through the bluebonnet infested cemetery."

"Wait." Fay said, turning back, "What if that's not a house? What if that was where they made these headstones?" She turned back to Jane, "and they're still making them."

"Well, that's a thought. I knew you weren't just a pretty face." She said turning back around before either could see the other blush.

During their walk they discussed different types of headstones and symbolism. They found an ornate cast iron grave covering. They also found both cats sunning themselves on a stone stadium chair and pillar near the back of the cemetery.

"This is why cats aren't allowed." Fay said in mock disgust. "We cannot take them anywhere." She continued .

Jane suppressed a laugh as both cats turned their heads to glare.

Heck stretched fore and aft saying, "It is us that takes you places, halfling."

"Only when we're being lazy, like now. Almighty goddess Hecate trapped in a cat's body."

"Your halfling is quite rude." Ebs stated matter-of-factly.

"Yes, I know." Heck said, narrowing her eyes at Fay, and opening a portal for the four of them.

Once they were back standing in the Parlor of McMortem's, Jane turned and asked, "Do you want to help me prepare the familiar's body for burial?"

Fay knew this was important, she didn't know why but she knew that how she answered was crucial, she looked Jane in the emerald eyes, "Absolutely, I want to be a part of it."

"Ok, follow me."

Once she entered the kitchen area Fay noticed several things. There was a wooden table with a black, cat size, casket sitting on it. White satin lined the casket, the smell of lavender seemed to permeate the room from it. There were fresh and dried flowers bunched on a table with a jar of water and the spell bag Jane had created the previous night, and the paw print they had made this morning. There were two collars, one that looked like an everyday use and one that looked more ceremonial. Along with everything else were a couple pictures of a gorgeous Siamese with a curly haired woman wearing glasses. Jane reappeared from where she had gone while Fay took everything in. Sara was following close behind her with a...

"Is that a miniature horse?" Fay blurted out.

Sara laughed, "Yes this is my familiar Connie, as in conquest."

Fay's smile grew, "as in the first horseman of the apocalypse." The small white horse whinnied and trotted in place at that. Fay's face blanked, went wide eyed, and she began laughing again. "She's wearing a hair bow... she's carrying a bow. Well played Sara, I knew I liked you."

"Thanks. Yes, my white horse Connie came in carrying a bow." She paused. "On her head but a bow, nonetheless. If the English language is going to use B-O-W to spell different things I feel I'm allowed to take liberties, besides it makes her feel pretty. Connie does serve a purpose though. We will be attaching a small cart to her, and she will bring the familiar to his final resting place."

"Oh wow." Is all Fay could muster.

"Ok now that you've met Con, we need to change into something slightly more appropriate for tonight's proceedings. Your T-shirt is better suited for cremations." Jane grinned at her.

Fay looked down at her shirt, "Oh yeah. I'll need to pop back to..."

"Do you really think I didn't pack you something?" Heck said, sauntering into the kitchen.

"There is no way for me to answer that without feeling your wrath."

"No. Your dress is upstairs."

Jane and Fay excused themselves upstairs while Sara excused herself to change. Heck and Connie stood in the kitchen having a silent conversation about humans. Fay topped the stairs and saw one of her favorite dresses waiting for her hanging from the bedpost. The dress was parchment colored with a pattern of roses, moths, spiders, and scorpions all in black. Just a touch of black lace embroidery around the edges along with a black shawl and leggings. There was a note pinned to it:

Should go fine with those damn Doc Martens you insist on wearing.

-H

Jane walked up behind her and laughed. "You've got your hands full."

"Clearly." Fay rolled her eyes. "Is this ok?" She gestured at the outfit.

"It's perfect." Jane said as she walked to the wardrobe and pulled out a black chemise, a black Victorian style ruffle shirt, and a thin silver band with three moons on it. "When we change, we should probably wipe down a little and envision wiping away the death energy we encountered today so we may focus on the death at hand. When we go back downstairs we will all go to the ancient ash tree in the way back and ground ourselves before preparing the body."

Fay looked at her a little confusedly but said "Ok." She grabbed her outfit and headed to the bathroom to wipe her death energy away. She stood there feeling disjointed staring at her deathling self in the mirror, trying not to overthink being birthed of death and how to wipe it away. And what would that make her if she did successfully wipe that part of her away? Her reflection was mocking her, and she began to panic when she heard a knock followed by a muffled but clearly amused voice.

"Listen halfling, I'm not asking you to be fully human."

Fay flung the door open in mostly mock outrage, "Did you just call me halfling?"

"Did it just pull you out of whatever weird spiral you were going down?"

"How did you... what do you mean?" Fay said quickly.

Jane rolled her eyes, "slipping on a dress and doing a quick wipe down of energy doesn't take ten minutes unless you're trying to wipe away half of the essence of who you are. All I meant was people like us attract and carry a lot of others with us and tonight needs to be about this soul. Now move so I can change." Jane finished, pushing Fay out of the bathroom, and shutting the door in her face with a cackle.

Fay went back to the bedroom to grab her shawl and leggings and put her Docs back on. Jane joined her a couple minutes later. They walked downstairs to find Sara wearing black flowing dress and a silver triple moon pendant around her neck.

"Shall we?" Sara asked, grabbing a jar of water. Connie on her heels, both Ebs and Heck sat gently atop the horse's back.

Fay and Jane followed. They walked toward the back of the property, past the crematorium to the edge of the woods that ringed the property. She heard Sara whisper something, *secret garden*, she thought, but immediately stopped pondering what had been said when the trees parted and there in front of them was a lit path into the woods. They walked down the thick lined narrow path of trees and vines to a clearing and the biggest ash tree Fay had ever seen. Fay turned in circles as the pathway closed behind them. Jane and Sara just watched her and smiled.

Jane looked at Fay and said," Ok halfling of death, I am trusting you with our piece of the tree of life, this is Ash."

Fay stared at the tree in awe, "Thank you."

At that the tree shifted and three seats appeared made from the trunk. Jane and Sara looked at each other and Fay noticed.

"What?" she asked

"Well, other than the three of us standing here there are only a smattering of other creatures that know about this place, our coven, their familiars, and their immediate family in some cases. Also, Ash has never made a chair for someone on the first meeting, so apparently you are quite special."

"I don't really know what to say to that." Fay looked a little spooked.

"Yeah, us either really." Jane admitted. "Let's take our seats and give Ash anything that we're still holding on to, let's clear our bodies and minds."

They all walked to the seats that had appeared in front of them. Followed by their respective animals. When Heck jumped into Fay's lap she glared at her and hissed, "Pull yourself together."

"What's going on? Did you know about this?"

"I don't know what's going on halfling, but we're here for it. It sounds like you might be able to check witch off on your bingo card though." Heck winked at her before curling up on her lap. Once Fay let herself feel the tree she began to calm, she could swear she heard the tree say, *do not fear my child you are just as much from life as you are of death. You belong here too,* it was so quiet though she could have imagined it. Just like that her eyes were open and when she looked around the others were stirring about.

Jane walked over to her and said, "I'm going to anoint your third eye with moon water. "We are of life and death. We belong to Ash and to Death Herself. And so, we drink." She anointed Fay's forehead and handed her the jar to drink from. She then knelt to Heck and repeated herself. Placing a drop of water on Heck's head and letting her drink from the jar cap. She then walked to the tree and walked clockwise around it whispering and pouring the water out evenly on the roots. After she finished, she walked back to the others and they made their way back down the reopening path to the house.

Once inside they began to prepare the body. Jane went to one of the freezers and asked Fay if she would carry the cat to the table next to the casket. Fay agreed and Jane pulled out a gorgeous and very cold Siamese. She very carefully set him on the table. Jane came over with another jar of moon water. We are going to wash him. She handed each of them a small cloth dipped in moon water, all three very gingerly wiped his beautiful fur down with it. Jane very carefully placed the ceremonial looking collar on the cat, then she gingerly picked him up and placed him in the casket and arranged all the flowers around him except for the one white lily. She placed the spell bag in front of his midsection and set the pictures in the back of the casket. Sara excused herself to get Connie ready. Once Sara was gone Jane studied Fay, "Are you ok?"

"I'm a little overwhelmed." Fay admitted.

"Yeah, I bet. I wasn't planning on taking you to Ash, at least not this soon, but she more or less demanded it."

"That doesn't sound ominous at all." Fay said

sarcastically.

"Did it feel ominous? Seriously?"

"No, not really."

"Ok then. I promise you we can talk about it as soon as we finish the service."

"Ok." Fay said with a small smile. "What's next?"

"We wait for Sara, and we wait for Lilith, his witch."She said looking back at the casket. "When Lilith arrives, she will place the lily, say a few words, and then we will close the casket and walk the procession out to his grave. Sara and I will walk in front leading the procession. Lilith will either walk next to or behind the casket, and I figured you could bring up the rear."

Sara walked back in with Connie pulling a beautiful cart with ornate filigree coming up about three inches off the base to encase the casket but not take away from it. The three of them carefully placed the open casket on the cart. Sara led Connie into the parlor to wait for Lilith.

"While I was hooking Con up, I placed the ramp so we're ready to go. Do you know what song she wants played?" Sara asked.

"Oh yes, she wants the instrumental version of Kitty, with the meows left in of course, by The Presidents of The United States of America."

"Seriously?" Fay asked before she could stop herself.

"Oh yeah, dead serious."

Just then there was a knock at the door.

"Come in." Jane said, gesturing with her hands.

The doors swung open and there on the threshold stood the curly haired woman from the pictures, wearing a well fitted black pant suit, with a ruffled sky blue shirt, a silver cat eye pendant, the eye the same color as the shirt, a top her head was a petite witch hat of the same fabric of her suit, her long pointy, curl toed, boots could be described as nothing other than witch boots.

"Hello Lilith." Jane said, momentarily grasping the woman's hand. "Are you ready to proceed?" She asked as she gave her the lily.

"As ready as one can be for this, I guess."

She approached the casket, petted her cat, placed the

lily in the casket, and said, "He left my life as he came into it, in a flash and with no warning. A few years ago he just ran up and jumped into my arms. Then a few days ago I came home, and he was curled up dead in the sink. He always was his own cat."

"He hasn't quite left." Jane said and pointed at her feet.

Everyone looked down to see a translucent cat with brilliant sky blue eyes sitting next to Lilith looking up at her.

"Of course not." Lilith smiled.

Jane and Sara closed the casket and placed another bunch of flowers on top of it. Sara whispered to Connie, and she slowly began to walk out of the house and down the ramp. Sara pressed something on her phone and quiet music began to play from the cart. The women walked in their places, with Fay bringing up the rear. She felt very protective of this scene, of this land. She felt as if her wings were extended fully to protect them, but knew better than to look, as she would only find disappointment.

They reached the small, prepped grave. Connie stopped and chuffed. Jane broke away and poured what looked like moon water around the edge whispering. Then she returned to the other women and said, "ready?" Looking at Sara and Lilith but sparing a quick smile for Fay. All three women stared at the casket, pointing their hands at it and whispered "up" in unison. The casket slowly began to levitate and was directed into the ground. Fay felt another surge of fierce protection course through and out of her.

Once the casket had been lowered, Lilith knelt and faced the ghost cat and spoke quietly, "I'm sorry this body was not strong enough to hold your beautiful soul in it any longer. You did good, stay if you wish, but please leave when you are ready." She kissed the essence of the cat's head and whispered. "Cover." A mound of dirt covered the small grave and Lilith stood with the ghost cat next to her and they all walked up the path toward the front of the house.

Fay stepped away into the parlor allowing Jane and Sara to finish their business. Jane was engrossed in conversation with Lilith, and Sara had wandered off into the darkness with Connie. Fay was sitting in the parlor when she could hear hooves and shoes approaching.

"Hey." Sara walked into the parlor.

"Hey."

"I can imagine today may have been overwhelming even being who and what you are." she paused as if trying to find words. "Your presence was felt and welcomed today, thank you for being here."

Fay looked at her strangely for a moment before realizing it was her turn to speak, "There is no place I would have rather been." And she meant it.

Sara smiled, "Good night Fay, I have to get this one home before she gets hangry and things get, well, apocalyptic."

Fay chuckled, "We do not want that."

Connie whinnied and walked out the door Sara leaving behind her with a small wave.

Not long after Sara left, Jane came in and saw Fay in a heap on the vintage sofa by the stairs. Jane quietly walked in and sat next to her, putting a hand on her leg. "Hey." She whispered. "Drained?"

"Yes. Very much so." Fay looked at her with dim eyes.

"Thought so. You were emanating a lot of energy."

"Was I?"

"Are you telling me you couldn't feel your own power? We all did. It felt like we had been encased by the strongest protection ward I've ever experienced."

"Oh that, yeah I felt it. I didn't really look too deep into it though." She looked at Jane then, searching her eyes. "Are you telling me I'm a witch?"

Dodging the question for a moment Jane handed Fay a piece of chocolate, "Here eat this. It will help. Let's get upstairs and change, then we can talk. I'm pretty drained too, and the comfort level of this hundred-year-old couch decreases exponentially after about thirty minutes."

Fay ate her chocolate and stood slowly. At that moment the cats appeared. "Let's skip the stairs." Hecate eyed Fay with a touch of concern. "You look like shit halfling, I think you may have overdone it."

"Thanks, cat, you always know the right thing to say to make me feel better." Fay's quiet voice dripping with sarcasm.

They moved around in silence getting ready for bed. Jane disappeared down the hall for a while. She reappeared as Fay was getting into the bed.

"I brought snacks. I figured we could use a little something. I also brought tea and water." She walked to the bed with a charcuterie board in hand while two cups of tea and two bottles of water hovered next to her. Fay reached out and grabbed her teacup and set it on the nightstand; then she took the tray from Jane and placed it in the middle of the bed. Jane took her teacup from the air and walked to the other side of the bed, letting both water bottles drop on the bed in between them. Jane settled and Fay immediately opened her mouth.

"No, eat." Jane said. "I will answer your questions as well as I can. No, I do not think you are a witch, exactly. I think it's possible that you have your own faery magic that you haven't learned to use and are beginning to tap into it now." Jane stopped for a bite of prosciutto. Then continued, "Not everyone called to Ash is a witch, not everyone in our coven, as it were, is a witch, some are faery folk."

"Ok." Fay said slowly. "What am I then?"

"My thought after tonight is that you are some kind of protector or guardian."

"What does that even mean?"

"We didn't mean to talk about you when you went inside."

"But you did." Fay said flatly.

"Well yes and I'm sorry. You kinda blew us all away. I'm not really sure how to say this because I'm not sure how you will react."

Fay rolled her hand with a I'm slightly annoyed and tired, get on with it gesture.

Jane sighed, "It felt like large dragon wings or something similar closed around us making us feel safe from all that might be wrong with the world." Jane hurriedly finished as she looked into Fay's eyes.

Fay had shifted imperceptibly but Jane noticed, she also noticed how cold Fay's eyes looked, and the wall that had closed in around her. "Like that, it felt like what you're doing right now, except from the inside. I'm telling you honestly, I have not told another person, no one, what very little you have said about your wings, it clearly pains you. It is also not mine to share. These were their own unpolluted perceptions. Fay, I promise you."

Fay's wings hesitantly unwrapped themselves from around her and her eyes grew warmer. "What does all this mean?" She whispered, looking even more exhausted.

"I really don't know. What I do know, is that I received a download that you were to be taken to meet Ash, and I know that I felt more protected than I have ever in my life as you stood watch over the burial proceedings."

"I am so tired."

"I know." Jane magically whisked away the dishes and closed the curtains with a "cocoon."

The Fourteenth of March

Fay found herself walking alone through the lawn of the stone maker's building outside the cemetery. She made the mistake of reading the names on the tombs: *Heck, Jane, Marie, Des-Ta-Toot, Sara, Connie, Ash*. She turned away from the stones having seen something in her periphery, an animal maybe. She turned back toward the building, quickening her step a bit. Once at the door she broke the barriers closing it off, ignoring the *No Trespassing* sign. She stepped lightly through the dilapidated building looking around trying to figure out why she had come here, when she saw a shadowy female with giant bat wings glide into view.

"Mother." She whispered angrily.

"Yes. Sorry for all the dramatics, but sometimes it seems like the only way to reach you. Speaking of dramatic, I see you've met your aunt, Ash Lifetree. The term Tree of Life was a mistranslation ages ago; she was just too polite to correct them."

"My what?"

"Your Aunt, I didn't realize a human body would make you this dense."

"I'm outta here. I'm waking myself up." Fay turned to leave.

"Please daughter. Wait. Your aunt is right. You are as much of the living as you are of death. You do not realize how much the living need you, and you the living."

"What in the cryptic fuck are you getting at?"

Fay woke sitting straight up in bed pouring sweat, "What the fuck?" She whispered to herself. She very gingerly slid off the bed, grabbed her notebook and tiptoed down the stairs. Heck was curled on the vintage sofa waiting for her. "Hey."

"Hello halfling."

"What the fuck is going on? Everything feels like we're spinning in a tornado."

"You've clearly been in Texas too long if you're saying tornado versus hurricane."

Fay glared at her, "If you'll recall my being here this long was not my idea."

"I don't know what's going on, but I know you will figure it out. You're not nearly as dense as your mother believes."

"Goddammit Heck. I knew you were creepin' in my dreams."

"It is part of my job to keep an eye on you and keep you safe. And for what it's worth I'm proud of you for calling her out on her cryptic messages. Now write in your damn notebook so we can both get some hopefully dreamless sleep."

March 14

*It's sometime after 3 am, and I'm sitting in the parlor of McMortem's
with Heck.*

I really don't even know where to start.

Today was so many things, but mostly confusing.

*So first both of our teams ended up going to the cemetery for a
couple of photo ops, but then the grims and crows went their own
ways. The cats stayed, sunning on a weird memorial. There was this
weird structure outside the cemetery. It looked like a house but I'm
pretty sure they made headstones there. The yard was full of carved
headstones, except when you went to touch them your hand went
right through. My concern is that the stone makers are trying to
correct their mistakes from the Otherside, I hope not, that would be a
terrible afterlife. That fucking house or whatever showed up in my
dreams, but I'll get to that insanity later.*

*Everything seemed ok until after we changed to take care of the
familiar's burial. Jane asked me if I wanted to be a part of the
process. Not only did I want to be part of it, but I felt I was supposed*

to be there.

First, I officially met Sara this morning. Then this evening I met Sara's familiar, Connie/ Conquest, named after one of the four horsemen of the apocalypse. When I realized she had placed a hair bow in the horse's mane I about died. Conquest rode in carrying a bow... a bow like to shoot people. Oh, the length she went for a pun. I'm not gonna lie- I was impressed.

They said they wanted to ground at the ash tree before preparing the body. I kept thinking I never saw an ash tree... that's when shit got really, really fucking weird. I followed them across the grounds past the crematorium toward the woods. As we approach the tree line a pathway lights up leading to a clearing beyond and to a gnarly ancient tree.

Jane said that there are very few that know about Ash, the tree of life. All either witches or magical creatures. I guess being half faery counts.

I thought she might be intimating that I was a witch as well at first, but she doesn't seem to think so. Heck will be so disappointed not to *be able to mark that on her "weird things about Fay" bingo card.*

When I sat upon the chair, which formed in the trunk of the ash tree,

this is what I felt more than heard: Do not fear me child, you are just

as much from life as you are of death. You belong here too.

I didn't tell Jane that part, I was too tired and overwhelmed.

The ceremony for the familiar was beautiful and I was honored to be

a part of the preparations and the ceremony. I felt very protective of

what was happening. I just didn't realize that all three witches felt it,

too. Jane said that all of them felt like they were encased in giant

dragon wings. I pretty much shut down at that, but Jane assured me

that she has never told anyone about my wings, that this was their

own words and feelings. WHAT THE FUCK?! I do believe her. I just

don't understand it. She thinks I am meant to be a guardian for the

living and the dead, whatever the fuck that means.

To top it off my dearest mother concocted an overly dramatic dream

scape to tell me that Ash Lifetree aka the tree of life is her sister, and

my aunt. When I reacted in a confused manner she insulted the

human form that she put me in and my intellect. I almost left then.

She stopped me and basically reiterated what Ash had whispered into my consciousness. Death Herself said to me "You are as much of the living as of death. You do not realize how much the living need you, and you the living."

I asked her what in the cryptic fuck was she getting at, and then I woke up.

Of course, Heck had been lurking in the shadows of my dreams and was down here in the parlor waiting for me.

So here I am awake.   Overwhelmed.   Confused.

Yet there is a sense of rightness.

-FF

When Jane woke, she knew she was alone in the bed before she even opened her eyes, and her heart twinged. "Goddammit." She muttered to herself. "Yeah, let's just add more to the pile you've dumped on her. Come to Austin, see what I do, meet the tree of life, be guardian of my coven, oh and by the way, I'm pretty sure I'm in love with you. Yeah, that will go over well." She muttered and buried her head in her pillow groaning, "Fuck." While Jane's head was buried, she felt the pressure of a cat land on her bed, which could have been living or a ghost. So, without unburying her face she said, "What?"

"She will come around."

"Heck? Oh, fuck did you hear my ramblings?" Jane said, looking up and then burying her face again in embarrassment.

"I did. And you shouldn't be embarrassed. I am just a cat after all."

"You are not JUST anything." Jane said, looking up to glare at Heck but saw a glimmer of slight amusement and compassion, and she softened her own eyes. "Her pain pains me. I feel the burdens she carries, including the one she least likes to acknowledge, and I do not wish to add to her burdens."

"I know. Just keep doing what you're doing. She will come around. She may not know what it is she feels for you, or maybe she is afraid to acknowledge it for fear of losing you. Who knows what goes on in that halfling brain of hers? Anyway, she is downstairs asleep on the couch in the parlor, and before you get any ideas, it's not because of anything you did."

"Thanks Heck." Jane said, opening the curtains, standing up and heading for the small kitchen to make coffee.

When Jane stepped out of the stairway, she looked over the back of the couch and saw Fay curled into the tightest ball asleep on the ancient thing. She quietly walked around and noticed Fay's notebook on the floor. She sat the coffee cups on the table in front of the couch and lightly sat on the edge.

"Hey." She said quietly, touching Fay's leg.

Fay woke with a start, blinked her eyes a couple times until she saw Jane and said, "Hey."

"I brought coffee."

"You're an angel."

"Nope, just a witch." She said smiling.

Fay smiled and sat up, "Thanks. My mother visited my dreams last night. I woke up rather abruptly, so I came down here. I didn't want to wake you."

"You could have, you know?"

"What?"

"Woken me up. I wouldn't have minded."

Fay looked at her as if the thought was ludicrous. "I didn't think we both should lose sleep that we desperately needed. I came down here. Heck and her lurking ways was waiting for me. I wrote for a minute and then I went back to sleep. Although I'm pretty sure there is a couch spring embedded in my ribs."

"There probably is. Have you had your tetanus shot recently? Do halflings need tetanus shots?" Jane laughed.

Fay rolled her eyes," I don't know if I need it, but I get

them either way, so no one suspects I'm anything but human."

"Apart from the lack of aging thing."

"You experience this as well, witch. We are not different in these things."

Jane just smiled like she had won an argument or something and then said, "Ready to head back to your place today?"

"Very much so. Not that I don't like it here..."

"But it was a bit much."

"Yeah," Fay said, looking a little embarrassed.

"Hey, it was a lot, definitely more than either of us had prepared for." Jane touched her leg again. "Seriously, it's okay. And if you want some time to yourself, I can stay here."

"No." Fay said quickly, looking a little surprised by her own reaction. "I, I don't know what's going on or how to explain. But I think we need to stay together. I feel this fierce need to protect, especially after last night. Not that I don't think you can take care of yourself, I just…" and Fay trailed off confused as to why she spilled so much thought vomit out in the open.

Jane just smiled and said "Ok."

They returned to Fay's house in late afternoon and decided to lounge about for the evening before resuming their tours of New Orleans cemeteries.

"I figured tomorrow we could hit Lafayette Cemetery #1 and bring home lunch from Commander's Palace. It won't be quite the same as eating there, but it's close. My favorite time to go is Halloween. They have a dress code, but on Halloween they are all about the shenanigans. We will have to go if it opens for Halloween."

"Sounds like a plan." Jane agreed, noticing but not reacting to the fact that Fay keeps making future plans for them.

"Want to watch a movie?"

"Sure."

"*Practical Magic*? Being at your house reminded me of that movie. Oh! And I can show you Sandra Bullock's witchy New Orleans home tomorrow."

"That's fine, as stereotypical as it may be, I love that movie. Although I may have an unpopular opinion about this movie."

"Really?" Fay was intrigued.

"Yes. Fuck the sisters. I want to be the aunts."

Fay laughed, "Oh, I think you are well on your way."

Fay curled up in her oversized chair with Heck. Jane was on the couch with Ebs. Nubs was also on the couch. Both crows stood on the mantle. This was clearly a popular choice with the harbingers. Even Claire showed as the title screen began to play.

"There is something other than food that can pull you away from true crime?" Fay looked at the dog with mock astonishment.

"Many things. Now are you going to scoot over and make room for me? Or are you going to make me sit on the floor." Fay scoffed but moved over so the large dog could fold herself into the chair. Claire made herself comfortable and Fay laid her head down on her.

Nubs scoffed in horror, "you let her use you as a pillow. That is so undignified."

Claire smiled at him showing all her teeth," Do I look like I'm trying to be dignified? You know Nubs, maybe she would like you as much as she likes me if you were a little less dignified."

Nubs chuffed, "my name is..."

"Yes, yes, Anubis. Point proven."

"Will you two please shut up?" Heck hissed.

The two women, still exhausted, fell asleep on their respective seats. After the movie ended Nubs went and sat in front of Claire who was stuck under Fay.

"Still feeling good about your choices?" He huffed at her.

Claire looked at him with bored eyes, "You know that stick you have wedged up your ass, you were supposed to fetch it, not sit on it."

Nubs began to growl, "How dare you!"

"I swear to me, if you wake them, Anubis, I will pull the stick out myself." Heck hissed. "And they say cats are catty. Geez you two." Nubs followed Heck out of the living room. "What is your deal with her?" Heck asked him.

"She doesn't take her job seriously."

"She doesn't take it seriously or as seriously as you?"

"What's the difference?"

"The difference is that NO ONE takes their job or anything else as seriously as you. No one!" Heck sighed, "you better figure out how to make peace with Claire because I have a feeling our teams are going to be intertwined."

"Why do you say that?"

"Are you really as dense as Fay? Look at them, really look."

He huffed at the insult, then his eyes went unfocused,

and he muttered, "God's bones, this is not good." When he really looked, he could see that even though the women slept across the room from each other their auras were touching.

"This may not be good for YOU, but it is for them. Get over yourself."

The great big grim huffed and lumbered right through the back door.

The Fifteenth of March

Fay woke up on her overstuffed chair early the next morning. Claire had somehow managed to sneak out from under her without waking her. She soon realized that there were cat eyes boring into her.

"What?" She whispered sleepily.

"Today is the 15th."

"Ookayy."

"Please tell me you know what the 17th is."

"Saint Gertrude's day? I mean I know she's the patron Saint of cats..."

"Wrong."

"Pretty sure it is."

"What else is it?" Heck growled.

"Um, the day of the Druid murdering douche canoe,

Saint Patrick."

"What else, halfling?"

"I don't know cat, what?"

"It is Jane's birthday you moron."

"Oh fuck, you're right."

"Yes, I know. You are definitely a moron."

"If I've said it once I've said it a thousand times. You always know just what to say." Fay glared at her.

"You're welcome." Heck said, making sure to let her back end linger in Fay's face before jumping down and wandering off.

Fay untangled her limbs from the blanket pretzel situation she was in. She looked at the defeated throw blanket and wondered how it had wronged her so much so that it must die. Then she continued on her way to the kitchen to start a pot of coffee. Things weren't much better in the kitchen. Her red coffee pot's digital clock glowed brightly with clear menace at her, 6:03 AM. "So not cool." She grumbled under her breath as she shuffled around. She walked into her bedroom to retrieve her notebook, only to find

Heck already asleep again, Nubs snoring in a most undignified manner, his head and paw on her pillow like a human. She glared then smiled, grabbing her notebook and backing out quietly. She then tip-toed back to the living room to grab her phone, tip-toed back to her room and snapped a quick photo and short video of Nubs, knowing how horrified he would be to be caught in such a position. Feeling quite proud of herself she shuffled back to the kitchen following the glorious smell of coffee, found a cup and shuffled to the small two seater table in the dining area.

March 15

It is hard on a humanoid ego to know that your cat, ancient goddess or not, is way smarter and more observant than you.

How have we known each other for years and yet, I have forgotten her birthday the one time we're actually going to be together for it. It's on a fucking holiday and like 2 weeks before my own.

Fuck.

My birthday is coming up. Cue existential dread and the birthed of death vortex. How did we get here? Where has the time gone?

I want to take her to Metairie to see the pale girl. I think she would enjoy that. Pack a picnic. Still, I need to think of a gift. It is too fucking early to think. I will figure it out. After mass quantities of caffeine.

It must be perfect.

Today we are going to walk through the Garden District, Lafayette Cemetery, and pick up food to take home to the crew from Commander's.

As much as I love Claire, I hope she isn't part of the crew this evening.

She and Nubs are two very different grims. I thought they might actually go at it last night. I love him, but Nubs has enough self-righteous dignity to elevate himself above the entire Orleans Perish, perhaps he would like the view from the vacant perch in what was Lee Circle. Ok I'm being rude, but it's been a rough couple of days and we were so tired. I thought I was gonna blow a gasket . Claire literally has zero fucks to give, unless it's to fuck with her compatriot, then she had all the fucks to give Nubs. It would be amusing if it didn't create so much tension.

Oh, speaking of amusing. Nubs is sleeping and snoring away in my bed with his head and paw on the pillow like a human. I got pictures and video. He will be horrified.

Fuck.

Maybe that's why I like Claire... different species... same cloth ... we're the same kind of jerk.

I've been in worse company.

Speaking of bad company, yesterday Jane offered to stay in Austin if I needed some space after everything that happened there...

And I blurted out all sorts of shit about needing to protect her and staying together!

Like WTF, who says shit like that. She came anyway. So I guess it's ok.

But for fuck's sake, reel it in FAY!

-FF

When Jane woke up on Fay's couch the first thing she noticed, other than the crick in her neck, was a cup of coffee on a warmer with a note:

I too know how to keep coffee warm.

-FF

Jane chuckled to herself and sat up reaching for the cup, bringing it to her face inhaling chicory, before taking a sip.

"Hey." Fay said to Jane's face full of coffee cup.

Jane gulped down the coffee, "Hey, I guess we will call it a draw on the coffee warming."

"I figure it's still witchcraft, I just bought mine from Amazon."

Jane laughed, "Touché. So, what's on the agenda for today?"

"Well, as soon as you're ready, I figure we will head to the Garden District. Since I've been up a while, I'm gonna take Heck and Nubs with me to check out Holt. We will probably be back in about thirty minutes."

"Ok, are you sure you don't want me to go too?"

"Nah. We won't be long. Enjoy your coffee."

"Ok." Jane settled into the couch with her coffee, Ebs came and curled up in her lap.

Nubs, Fay, and Heck walked through the portal and in the gates of Holt. Fay walked slowly through the cemetery, reaching out, feeling for anything off or out of sync, but it didn't feel any more out of sync than usual.

"Everything seems to have calmed down. I think it was just an episode of blurred lines." Heck reported to her as they traipsed through the tall grass toward the crematorium.

"Ok, yeah it feels like it's normal weird to me as well. What about Des?"

"Still M.I.A. but again, all the taphofae say that's not really that unusual."

"Right." Fay agreed, still feeling a touch uneasy. "Do you have anything to add, Nubs?"

"He just wants to stop patrolling here, he has more important things to attend to."

Nubs gave her a look that had the air of a Victorian

poisoner as if to say, I am an upstanding member of society, but I will put arsenic in your tea.

Fay caught the look and asked, "What have you been up to while we're on hiatus? I notice you disappear at times." Nubs continued to stare daggers at Heck. Heck for her part, continued to focus on anything but him.

"He has been grimming outside of hospitals with known critical Corvid patients and nursing homes." Heck said with an air of nonchalance.

Fay turned on him, "Seriously? You have ignored a direct order from Death Herself? For what? Because you can't not work? You carry on with your pompous attitude toward the rest of us, especially Claire, and you're the one breaking the rules! You are way more arrogant than I could have imagined. I personally couldn't care less if you carry on with pacing outside the buildings of the dying, if Death Herself does she will make it known, hopefully with a night in the Perish Pound to knock you down to our level, but you need to stop with this attitude. You act like the rest of us aren't doing important things."

"Yes, showing your girlfriend cemeteries is very important." He grumbled.

Fay just glared at him a moment, anger simmering in her darkened eyes and said with dead calm, "Showing my friend the history of death and culture in our city is important. Helping Jane bury a witch's familiar is important. These are things of interest to us and helps us be well-rounded death workers." Fay finished.

Nubs stared at her seemingly nonplussed, "Yeah, friend, keep telling yourself that." And he lumbered into the shadows of a tree and was gone.

Fay watched him leave then she turned on Heck and glared," Are y'all planning our fucking wedding or something?"

"No." Heck said calmly, "But I call dibs on flower girl."

Fay meant to yell but only got as far as, "you want to be the..." and burst out laughing picturing the ridiculousness of Heck in a dress with a tiny basket of flower petals. "I hate you."

"No, you don't. Are you satisfied with our walkabout?"

"Yeah, I guess, something just seems off."

"This place always seems off."

"True." Fay agreed as they walked through the portal and into the living room.

"How was your survey of Holt?" Jane asked, now fully dressed, sitting on the couch with Ebs.

Fay shot a look at Heck, "Enlightening." She continued without elaborating, "Ready to start our adventure?"

"Sure." Jane said, also glancing at Heck, who winked at her. "Where is Nubs?"

"Fulfilling his life mission to scare the bejesus out of the dying even when he's been told to stand down. Apparently, he's just that passionate about his work."

"Oh shit." Jane looked at her flabbergasted.

"Yes, I guess that's why he's so irritated with the rest of us because we didn't defy a direct order and continue on with our calling." Fay made air quotes and rolled her eyes.

"Yeah, that's it." Heck muttered and more loudly, "Ready?" As she opened a portal to the Garden District.

Fay shot Heck a much less passive I'm going to kill you look than Nubs had given her. She was met with the biggest, most innocent looking golden eyes from Heck. Fay scoffed and walked through the portal, Jane already through and waiting.

"This!" Fay twirled on a raised piece of sidewalk with exaggerated hands, "is where the rich people live. And this, that I am standing on, is a carriage block." Jane just stared at her so she continued in animated fashion. Fay jumped off the block, "It is so that when fanciful southern ladies would leave their home they did not have to drag their long hoopy dresses through the muck of New Orleans streets. Instead, they would gather said hoopy skirts, making sure to not even show an ankle, and be mistaken for a harlot mind you, and step upon this block and into the waiting carriage." Fay finished with a flourish now back on the block.

"Ankle harlot, really?" Jane mused.

"Oh yes we take ankles very seriously in these parts." Fay said with all the seriousness she could muster.

Jane arched an eyebrow, "How seriously?"

Fay ignored her, turning away as her cheeks reddened, "If you will follow me, I will show you where Anne Rice used to live, where John Goodman does live, and of course the real reason we are here, Sandra Bullock's witchy abode."

"Witchy?"

"You'll see."

They walked through the Garden District. Jane found herself bewitched (as it were) by all the historic mansions, and old trees. Finally, they approached a house with a high steeped roof and spires, lots of intricate wrought iron, and gingerbreading. "This is Sandra Bullock's house." Fay gestured in front of them.

"Whoa! That is definitely some *Practical Magic* shit right there."

"I told you. This architecture is purely for aesthetics in this part of the world. The high sloping roof and spires are more prominent in places where it snows heavily, they serve no purpose other than to look pretty and witchy here." They stared in awe for a few moments and carried on to Lafayette Cemetery.

"So, the cemetery has been closed a while for renovations." Fay air quoted, as she unlocked the gate and they slipped in unnoticed. As soon as Fay had locked the gate and they turned to explore there was a flamboyantly dressed taphofae in their space.

He wore brightly colored wrap pants, no shirt over his dark muscled skin, and his head wrapped in a scarf. "Ooh Fay, baby girl, where you been?"

"Hey Ellis, I've been around."

He looked Jane up and down, "I see dat baby girl."

Fay gestured to a blushing Jane, "This is my friend Jane."

"She shore is, baby girl, she shore is." Then addressing Jane, "How do sugar, I is Ellis, Keeper of Lafayette Cemetery #1, and diner in da dumpster of Commander's. Dis is da best gig. Though there is da homeless here now. Gots da share."

"Homeless?"

"Yeah, baby girl, just finished tellin' dat wolfman bout dem."

"Wolfman?"

"Yeah, dat reaper man."

"Oh, Wolf?"

"Yeh he shore do growl, told me to mind my own B. I say okay I be here mindin' it. I sure like when ya visit doh, no growl from baby girl or sugar Jane." He flitted about them.

"Thanks Ellis, we're gonna walk around for a while and I'll bring some fresh soup for you after we hit Commander's when we're done."

"Ooh child, you stop now. You speakin' Ellis' language." He beamed and flittered off.

"He's fun." Jane beamed at her.

"Yes, I'm quite fond of Ellis, I'm surprised he didn't tell you his French joke."

Just then, the faery clearly not out of ear shot, flitted back into their space, "Oh baby girl, I plum forgot." He turned to Jane as Fay rolled her eyes,"Sugar, I stays away from da French Quarter. Do ya know why? Do ya know why faeries don't like da French?" he asked seriously.

Jane shook her head. So did Fay but in defeat already knowing what was to come.

"Cuz sugar, they et tu fae." He flitted around them quite proud of himself and flew off for real this time.

Jane was laughing so hard she was crying, "that was hilarious."

"Don't encourage his horrid puns." Fay said, staring off after him. Then more seriously, "I find his comments about Wolf odd. I would hate to find out he was faephobic."

"It's always disappointing to find out things like that about someone you know."

"Indeed. Ok, come on I've gotta show you something. You have a crypt here."

"I have a what?"

Fay grinned and grabbed her by the arm, leading her down the tree root covered path and into the maze of tombs. Finally reaching the tomb she was looking for she proudly pronounced, "Ta-Da!" While doing her best Vanna White impersonation.

Jane stared at the tomb then she stared at Fay. "Really? Gay Jane? You've lost your mind." She said, the smile she was fighting back slipping out as she spoke.

"Well, you're gay and your name is Jane… So… I feel there's a strong argument for this tomb belonging to you." Fay said with a shrug.

"I'm not sure if this is more or less unbelievable than the Funk grave." Jane said, shaking her head.

Fay smiled and they continued on walking in silence for a bit until Fay noticed a bone sticking out of one of the coping graves. "Look, this happens on occasion, a bone will surface."

"Yikes."

"Yes it can be a little surprising the first couple of times."

Jane looked at her, a little bit of intrigue and a little bit of horror in her eye, "How often does it happen?"

"Here, not often. Holt however…" she trailed off and they continued walking. Fay finally built up all of the courage she didn't have and said, "So your birthday…" she paused as Jane looked at her. "Is there anything specific you would like to do?"

Jane didn't quite make eye contact and hesitated when she said, "Yeah maybe, but..."

"But what?" Fay asked cautiously.

"Can we go to Saint Roch?"

Fay tried to unsuccessfully hide a facial twitch, she took a deep breath before answering, "Can we maybe make a compromise? The reason I hesitate is that it's a 50/50 chance of what mood I'll be in when I leave that place. I don't want to risk being a sourpuss on your birthday, we've got Heck for that. What if I take you to Saint Roch tomorrow, and I surprise you for your birthday?"

"So, your idea of a compromise is Saint Roch early, plus a surprise the following day? Deal!" She said enthusiastically. "And thank you."

Fay smiled and promptly changed the subject, "Are you getting hungry? I'm ready to get our food and head home if you are."

Jane nodded but her eyes sparkled as if she were trying to figure out the surprise.

"You won't figure it out." Fay said confidently.

Jane glared.

They crossed the street to Commander's and immediately noticed what appeared to be a group of homeless and a few stray dogs waiting for handouts from restaurant. "This is weird." Fay said. "So many homeless in the affluent neighborhood."

"Maybe they're migrating to open restaurants."

"Yeah maybe." Fay said, looking around concerned. "I called in the to-go before we left the house. Salmon BLTs, turtle soup, and the best pecan pie known to human and faery kind as far as I'm concerned."

"Turtle what now?"

"You heard me, and you have to try some. I gotta take some to Ellis before we go."

"He can have mine." Jane offered selflessly.

"There's plenty." Fay countered, retrieving their heaping bags of food.

Ellis saw them enter the gates, and he fluttered over at

top speed. He landed next to Fay as she knelt to open the bag, one of the quarts of soup, plastic ware, and two portion cups. She used a plastic spoon to fill one of the portion cups and handed it to the faery. The faery took flight around them, "You shore do know how ta treat a man baby girl, too bad we play on da wrong teams, if ya know what I mean." He then did a couple of pelvic thrusts in the air and winked at her just in case she was unsure.

"You sure are feisty. Anyone you want to share this with? I have another container."

"I been tryina get Duckie boy ta see me, dis jus' might do. He not much for dumpster dinin'."

"So, you think if I cut a sliver of the pie, it would sweeten the deal?"

"Ooh ooh baby girl I love me some pee-CAN pie." Fay finished plating food for the faery and the two turned to portal home and could hear Ellis, "Bye baby girl, bye sugar Jane, you shore is sweet to bring me dis food."

They smiled at each other as they landed back in Fay's house.

The whole of both crews (minus the beetles) were there. Everyone put differences aside for Commander's lunch, even two stubborn grims.

"Yuck." Jane exclaimed, having dipped a spoon in the soup container.

Fay chuckled, "You should see your face."

"More for us." Heck Said casually waiting for Fay to make her a bowl of soup and a chunk of salmon and bacon. "Oh, great havers of thumbs, can you help us poor thumbless folks out?" Heck asked impatience oozing from her being.

"I guess, since you asked so nicely." Fay glared at her but started plating food for the crew. The animals stayed in the kitchen as Fay and Jane took the plates to the small dining room table.

"Well, the salmon is fantastic...and this PIE! It's otherworldly. The only thing questionable is the soup, but that's clearly a me issue since everyone else in the house enjoys it!"

"Oh, it's definitely you." Fay laughed.

Jane just flipped her off and kept eating her pie.

They relaxed the rest of the evening until Jane announced that she was going to soak and go to bed, in a bed this time and not all pretzeled on a couch. Fay decided to stay up a while, and as soon as she heard water running, she motioned for Heck to come to her. She quickly recapped the birthday compromise and plans.

"Good call about Saint Roch." Heck agreed.

"So I have an idea for a gift, can you reach out to Sam and ask him to bring his wares?"

"Oh yes, I can go now, what a wonderful idea." Heck said.

About thirty minutes later Heck came bounding through her own portal with a small faery dressed in complete pirate regalia riding on her back. "Good day, Fay."

"Good day, Sam. Sorry to trouble you at this hour, but I might be interested in purchasing some of your wares." She replied automatically, and smiled, as it had not been day for some time.

"Aye, your beastie said this was a booty call, so, I

brought many shiny things. Though I don't like to part with my trey-sure."

Fay spared a glare for Heck before responding, "Yes I know, you come by your booty honestly. I wish to bargain with you for it, not take it."

He opened up his leather bag and started pulling bits out, "Aye. Here are three pendants I have made of broken stained glass from a tomb in Metairie, only scavenged when they were to be replacing the window."

"Of course."

"I have coffin nails, bent into small rings or charms. I also have dried flower petals pendants made from flowers left at the tombs on Metairie. Lemme see what else." he said falling into his bag.

Fay leaned over and righted the faery, "I like this one", she said, picking up a piece of blue and white jagged stain glass, with seven points, like an abstract faery star. Sam had carefully encased it in silver with a small hoop for a chain or piece of leather. "What would you like for it?"

The faery sat for a moment thinking. "Three coins of your choosing. A thimble of coffee, a crumble of pecan pie, and a bit of soup."

"Deal." Fay smiled, "Have you talked to Ellis today?"

"No, but I did see Duckie on his way to see Ellis."

"I see. Well, let me gather your payment."

"Aye, my lady. I shall entertain myself by riding your beastie some more."

"Ok, but be quiet about it. This is a surprise." She said, glancing toward the closed bathroom door.

The faery mimed locking his lips and threw the key into his bag. Then he ran at, and jumped on Heck's back. Fay suppressed a laugh as she went to put together a care package for him. She kept portion cups for such occasions. She filled one with pie, one with coffee and one with soup. She then went and rummaged through her change drawer and pulled out a wheat penny, a Canadian 20 cent coin, and a Kennedy half dollar. She walked back into the living room just as Heck deposited the faery back at his bag.

"Will your bag hold all this?"

He eyed the portion cups and coins in her hands, "Aye my lady. You are too kind."

"I don't believe so. I respect your work both as a taphofae and as an artist. I will be at Metairie with a friend the evening after next, will I see you?"

"Aye, we have a meeting of the taphofae in the afternoon. Scheduling for Holt until Des returns but I should be back by nightfall."

"Great, will you show us which tomb the glass came from for the pendant?"

"Aye, my lady, until then." He bowed, heaved his now bulging bag up and jumped onto Heck's back just as she made a portal and jumped through.

Fay shook her head and smiled at the unlikely duo. They really were quite fond of each other. She pocketed the pendant still shaking her head when Heck reappeared alone. "Back so soon?"

"Yeah. I love him but he wears these old paws out."

Fay and Heck curled up in the oversized chair. Fay with

her notebook in hand.

March 15 continued...

Today was a very enlightening day to say the least. After coffee this morning, I went with Heck and Nubs to Holt and did a walk through. Everything seems ok there or as ok as it ever is.

The enlightenment came from Nubs. He apparently feels such a calling to do his job, that he sees fit to disregard a direct order from Death Herself. He's been grimming the shadows outside the hospitals and nursing homes.

What the actual fuck?!?!

He accused me of not doing anything other than courting Jane. Our outings have been pleasurable but also educational.

Speaking of outings she wants to go to St Roch for her birthday which is a terrible idea, since it will put me in a terrible mood. So, I made a compromise and we're going tomorrow and I'm surprising her on her birthday.

Anyway, back to today. We went to The Garden District to ooh and ahh at all the rich and famous' abodes. Then we walked through Lafayette Cemetery where she met Ellis. It always amuses me that

Ellis guards that cemetery because he reminds me of the character Lafayette from the TV show True Blood. It makes me wonder if one of the writers met Ellis, it's rare but not unheard of.

I picked up lunch from Commander's, shared it with our faery friend. Ellis said he had seen Wolf around and it sounded as if Wolf was rather rude to him. I find that disconcerting. I hope he was maybe just being gruff and isn't faephobic. That would be quite upsetting to find out, being half faery myself. I will never understand people who think one magical or non magical creature is more or less than themselves. It was strange to see so many homeless so near Commander's, so near the affluent, I'm sure they will have them moved out of the neighborhood. Again, people thinking they're better than.

One really great thing about today is that I figured out what to get Jane for her birthday and it goes perfectly with my plans. I had Heck ask one of my favorite (and Heck's) faeries to come see me and bring his jewelry. Sam did not disappoint. He never has. He brought me a nice selection, but he also brought the perfect piece. A pendant from broken stained glass in Metairie (that was replaced) it's a seven point shard of blue and white opaque glass, with faery crafted silver

encasing it. He did an impeccable job on it. All it cost me was a

portion cup filled with soup, one filled with coffee, and one filled with

pie, and three coins. He of course felt I over paid and I felt it was a

steal. He is supposed to show us where it came from on the 17th.

The best thing about Sam coming around though, is his relationship

with Heck. They're an odd couple for sure. She lets him ride her calling

her "beastie" and she scampers around trying to buck him off,

sometimes when they really get going, she will portal in and out of

places, I'll have no idea where she's gone and then boom they're

back. Seeing her cut loose a little is good for my soul so it must be

great for hers.

Tomorrow will most likely be draining. I better get to bed

... there's already a witch asleep in it.

I like it... I've gotten quite used to not sleeping alone...

Well, I never really sleep alone with the animals always around

But you know what I mean...

Self.

(Yes keep talking about yourself to yourself as if explaining yourself

to you. That definitely won't look insane if someone finds this)

I am clearly tired.

-FF

The Sixteenth of March

Jane woke up early and was too excited about the day's adventure to Saint Roch to go back to sleep. She knew it was a huge deal for Fay to take her there. She had half expected her to say no when she asked, so she found herself deeply touched to know Fay trusted her enough with this. She knew, for Fay, this place simultaneously represented loss and connectedness. With thoughts wandering she got up and started coffee; she and Ebs portaled back to her place to get some lavender syrup and came right back. It was a lavender coffee kind of day. She started cooking a scrambler with eggs, bacon, potatoes, spinach, and cheese. Apparently, that was the cue for the entire house to wake. They all trudged into the kitchen like bacon zombies following their noses.

"What smells so good?" Fay shuffled sleepily from the master into the kitchen.

"Scrambler. Here, try this." she said, thrusting a mug into Fay's hands.

"Why isn't it black?"

"Just fuckin' try it." Jane shot back.

Fay took a tentative sip, followed by a gulp, "That's strange and delightful, kinda like yourself. What is it?"

Jane just barely suppressed a blush, and said, "Arsenic." With a conspiratorial smile.

"Fuck! Well at least it tastes good." Fay said, taking another swig.

"Go sit. I'll bring food in a sec, and to answer your question it's lavender and vanilla almond milk. You're welcome."

"Is the lavender to hide the arsenic?"

"Obviously." Jane said exasperated.

They ate and dressed. Fay tried to prepare herself for the coming day. She couldn't quite believe she was taking someone to a place only Heck had gone to with her. She thought about all that Jane had shared with her the past few days, and she realized she wanted to let her into this most inner sanctum even as it weighed heavy on her mind and soul. Fay tried to not look uneasy about their adventure as she asked, "You ready?"

"Yes." Jane said with a comforting smile, but her eyes betrayed her excitement.

"Come on then." Heck said creating a portal.

They landed on the sidewalk just outside of Saint Roch Cemetery #2, and Heck sauntered off. "Saint Roch is split into two cemeteries, let's start here and work our way over to #1, and the chapel." Fay said, thinking to herself, bless that damn cat. They began walking through the cemetery. There was quite the mix of family tombs and coping graves. Fay showed her her favorites, like the coping grave with a huge horse head as part of the wall. The statue of the cherub that wasn't cute and sweet looking, but looked more like he walked out of a burning building ready to fight. It was such an absurd thought that they created a whole action movie, Cherub Man. "He looks like a cherub, but he's really a shrunken angel out for justice or revenge! No one really knows because no one will watch this awful plot of a movie!" Fay declared in her best movie announcer voice. Jane laughed until she snorted, and then they both began to laugh again. As they laughed along, the angel's face seemed to soften into a smile behind them.

Once they calmed down and caught their breath they continued to stroll through the cemetery. When they rounded a corner and saw a spot in the pavement where, *At Rest*, was spelled out in tiles, it stopped Jane in her tracks. "Oh wow."

"Yeah, they're like the street tiles in the French Quarter, only sepia. Custom job for sure. Though I have seen the blue street tiles used on graves before."

"Why am I having deja vu looking at this?" she muttered thoughtfully, then her eyes brightened, "This is the print above your bed!"

"Indeed, it is." Fay smiled.

"The cemeteries here definitely have their own look and feel."

"They do, here check this out." Fay said, grabbing her by the hand and pulling her along. "The mosaic on this family tomb was blessed by the pope. Plaque and everything."

"How does that work exactly?" Jane said pretending

not to notice the hand holding, since it appeared Fay didn't realize she was still holding on to her.

"I dunno! I'm not Catholic!" Fay said in mock exasperation, throwing both hands up in the air.

Jane just laughed at her, "My apologies."

"Well, I guess it's time to go see the main attraction, #1 and the chapel to see where I keep my drama and dismay locked away." Fay said dramatically

Jane literally choked on her own spit at that, "Oh dear, your drama is not locked away, it roams quite freely." She said gesturing her hands at and around Fay's person.

Fay shot her a look, "Come on, you."

They walked around #1 for a bit before Fay said, "Ok, let's go in." They silently slipped into the chapel and made their way to the shrine of Saint Roch. The walls and shelves of the small room were covered with prosthetic legs, polio braces, hands, teeth impressions, crosses, statues, and rosary beads. There was one curious spot on a sturdy shelf next to the window with just enough room for a person to sit. Fay walked directly to the spot, and sat, false toes dangling next to her head.

Jane looked around in awe, a touch of unease possessing her, "Why, why here?"

Fay looked at her with a pained expression grasping her own arms, "I feel I belong here." She sighed and continued, "it reminds me that I am half human, and that some of those humans know the pain I feel. I can fucking feel them, like phantoms tethered to my back." She said through gritted teeth as her neck muscles spasmed, swiping at tears. She was shocked at how angry she felt, but they hurt today and she was feeling awfully exposed at the moment.

Jane took a tentative step toward her, "Please tell me about them. Your wings."

"There's not much to tell, I see them in glimpses on occasion, I could see them more clearly as a child, so I've always known. I vaguely remember them being bat-like, so, dragon is not that far off. I remember seeing them in the mirror when I was really young and thinking I might be a vampire or something, I'm pretty sure I looked for fangs. I, of course, asked Marie if I was a vampire."

She laughed without humor, "Marie obviously clarified that I was in fact not a vampire, which I'm pretty sure I was disappointed about at the time. She always told me my wings are not meant for this realm, that is why they are so hard to see." Tears were streaming now. "I've never felt whole. I'm not quite human, and I don't know what one would call a wingless faery other than broken." She hung her head, refusing to make eye contact, "broken, like the people that wore these." She gestured vaguely and then clung to herself again, still not looking up. So, she was quite surprised when she felt hands on the side of her face, and could see shoes facing her.

"Look at me." Jane whispered. Fay slowly obeyed. "I know how hard it was to bring me here, to show me this most vulnerable part of yourself, your pain, your doubt. You are the strongest creature I know, broken, and partial as you feel, power and strength exude from your very soul, I felt that and those elusive wings of yours the other night. It's one of the things I love about you. Thank you for bringing me here, I'm not sorry to be here, but I am sorry to have caused you pain." She kissed her forehead and moved to step back and give her some space. Thinking to herself, did I say love?

Fay reached for her, "Don't." She said barely above a whisper. Thinking to herself did she say love?

Jane stepped back into her space "Ok, I'm here."

"I'm sorry I'm such a mess. The only one who has ever accompanied me here is Heck, and she doesn't really give me a choice. Not even Màrie has come here with me. I have never shared this much of myself with anyone, and I'm a little scared."

"That's ok too. We have known each other for ages but have never shared space the way we have as of late, and well, our connection can be a little overwhelming."

"For you too?" Fay asked, not quite meeting Jane's eyes.

"Yes." Jane said, hugging Fay's slumped form. What she didn't expect was for Fay to wrap her black ink and porcelain arms around her, still crying. They stayed like that for a long time. Fay sitting, burrowed into Jane, arms around her waist and

Jane standing over Fay, arms around her shoulders, cheek pressed to the top of Fay's head. Heck sat just outside the door waiting with a look of cautious delight on her face. After a long while Jane asked, "Do you want to go home?"

Fay just nodded.

As if on cue and not as if she had been lurking, Heck appeared in the doorway.

"Come on, let's go." Jane coaxed

Fay stood and walked still holding on to Jane through the portal. They walked straight into Fay's bedroom where the door was already shut, and pajamas laid out. On top of Fay's pajamas was a typed note:

You did good today. Rest.

-H

Fay fought back tears, her eyes already swollen, and climbed into the bed and Jane's arms before falling asleep.

March 16

Everything has changed.

Fuck!

It's about 11pm and I just woke up with Jane's arms wrapped

protectively around me as if she were the one with wings.

I let her in

And she didn't run

She didn't shy away from my wounds.

She embraced them.

Yet here I am fighting the urge to run

And the urge to kiss her.

I don't know what to do.

What if it's too much?

She did refer to our connection as overwhelming.

What if this messes up our friendship?

What if I fuck it all up?

Jesus Christ, I just looked up and Heck is glaring at me. She's either reading my mind or can see through the pages to what I've been writing.

If an archeologist finds this one day, I hope they understand how awful it is to have a long living, talking, literate cat...

She definitely knows what I'm writing.

I think I'll be safer if I put this down and go back to sleep.

-FF

The Seventeenth of March

The next morning Fay woke before Jane, determined to be in a good mood and not let her over thinking brain ruin Jane's birthday. She was quite surprised when she looked at her phone and it was after 10 am, she extracted herself from the bed and Jane's protective grasp on her shoulder. She walked into the kitchen sleepy eyed to make coffee.

"You better not." Heck hissed.

"Goddammit." Fay yelped. "You scared me."

"Yes well, you need to shut your brain up. Do not allow yourself to ruin the best thing to ever happen to you. I know you're scared, love is that way sometimes. And before you argue, you love her, and before you argue, she loves you. Neither of you want to be apart now that you're together. I can speak as an objective observer."

"Can you though?"

The cat just glared at her. "Don't make me kill you and eat your eyeballs. Not today, not on Jane's birthday."

"Well, yes, I could see where that would ruin the day." Fay continued moving about the kitchen ignoring the glaring eyes of her cat. She made herself a cup of coffee and turned on Heck. "Look, you psycho, I'm gonna go shower and throw some clothes on, will you please portal me to the store to pick up some picnic items."

"Please wear something decent."

"I'll take that as a yes, you will." Fay turned on her heels and strode into the bathroom shutting the door. She returned about 30 minutes later in a black cotton dress with little white stars all over it and her Docs. Her blond hair still damp.

"I guess you look ok." Heck mused.

"Thanks. Too bad the hair drying witch is still asleep. I didn't want to run the hair dryer and risk waking her." Fay said, explaining her wet hair.

"Have I been summoned?" A sleepy voice said, trailing

a hand down Fay's long hair, drying it as she went.

Fay turned, "Thanks, is that how someone summons a witch?" She kissed her cheek briefly and said, "Happy Birthday." And stiffened slightly as her brain caught up with what she had done so casually.

Jane smiled slightly, but otherwise ignored both gestures, "Thanks, and no or I don't think so, witches aren't usually summoned, that's usually reserved for demons."

"There's coffee, and speaking of demons, Heck and I are going to grab a few things at the store. Need anything?"

"Ooh maybe like a raspberry Danish or something."

"As you wish." Fay said as her and Heck vanished through the portal.

They were only gone for about forty minutes. Returning with Danishes, a bag with meats, cheeses, and garlic bread, a sparkling sweet white wine. And the saddest long-stemmed red rose Fay could find. As she was putting things away

Jane appeared in the kitchen fully dressed in black skinny jeans, a white peasant blouse, sparkly Docs, and a black felt hat.

"What'd ya bring me? Jane asked jokingly.

Fay turned and stared for a moment before coming to her senses, "A box of assorted Danishes, including but not limited to raspberry, and this rose."

"Thank you on both accounts, but why this particular rose?" She was gently turning it in her hands and looking at the darker red and dry petals.

"Because it's broken, and you're good with broken things."

"I see. Thank you." She said with a knowing smile. "So, what's the plan?"

"The plan is to break open this box of Danishes with another cup of coffee. Then nothing until about 5 pm. Is there anything specific you would like to do today?"

"Nope, we did what I wanted yesterday."

They ate their Danishes, once finished they located a vase for Jane's morose rose. They milled about, turning on the TV and watching the news for a bit, realizing quickly what a horrible idea that was. As they spent the day doing nothing together, there seemed to be an unspoken knowledge between them that while the world at large was quite literally plagued, they had found something truly incredible, each other. Around four in the afternoon, Jane went to freshen up while Fay began preparing their light picnic of meats, cheese, bread, and wine.

As the clock crept toward five Fay asked Jane, "Are you ready? I want to share something special with you on your birthday. My favorite cemetery, both in the light and the dark." She grabbed Jane's hand and nodded at Heck who opened a portal for them to walk through. They stepped on to perfectly manicured grass next to a small stream where ducks swam. She deposited their picnic basket next to a tomb and turned to Jane, "This is Metairie Cemetery." Fay said gesturing with her hands as she twirled around."

"This place is gorgeous." Jane said in awe.

"We could be here all day and I couldn't show you all the beautiful things here." Fay reached for her hand, "Come on."

They walked hand in hand down the paved path talking about the symbolism and architecture of the tombs, the beautiful stained glass in many of the tombs. And the gaudy audaciousness of a few of the mausoleums. Fay took her to the Pyramid shaped Brunswig Mausoleum, and as advertised, it put the pyramid in Saint Louis #1 to shame. They walked and talked for a couple of hours taking in the magnificent mausoleums and stunning stained glass. They came to the crypt housing the Angel of Grief, and Fay urged Jane to look through the hole where the stained glass was broken.

Jane peered in and her breath caught, "She is so beautiful."

"According to Sam, the taphofae here, her name is Emelyn. My understanding is that many of the statues in the cemeteries are inhabited, but not all. I've never seen them move, but I have questioned whether they were facing that direction when I had looked at them last."

"Seriously?"

"Dead serious." Fay smiled wryly.

Jane rolled her eyes, "that actually explains a lot."

"Come on, the sun will set soon and I have dinner and a show, of sorts, planned." Fay gave her a wry smile and grabbed her hand, as Jane looked at her with a touch of uncertainty.

They headed back toward the front of the cemetery and the tomb with the surname of Rice, that they had portaled next to earlier. Fay unfolded a blanket and unpacked the picnic she had left behind. They sat down close together on the blanket. Right before the sun dipped below the horizon Fay said, "I have something for you." She pulled the pendant, now on a simple leather cord, out of her small dress pocket. "This is a broken piece of stained glass from one of the tombs, Sam fashioned this pendant with faery silver, he's supposed to be around later to show us where it came from. I picked this one because it reminded me of a faery star which is…"

"Said to be a portal to the Otherside." Jane finished, looking down at the pendant in her hand, eyes glassy with tears unable to speak anymore. Fay took an unseen deep breath, she cupped Jane's chin gently pulling her face up and kissed her. They sat there like that for a few moments, tears of joy finally spilling from Jane's eyes. They were so captivated by each other in that moment, that they did not notice the shadow slink across their path and disappear amongst the adjacent tombs.

Fay finally broke the kiss and spoke a little breathlessly, "I don't want to stop kissing you, but… there's a spirit I want you to see." Fay's eyes lit up. "Look." Fay pointed down the path just as a ghostly little girl appeared and began walking toward them. She looked around as if in awe of the beauty around her until she reached the tomb they were sitting by. The girl walked through the iron gate that swung open as she approached, knocked three times, and disappeared within the tomb.

"Holy sh…." Jane said.

"Yeah." Fay agreed. "I'm not sure, but I feel she is lost in some way. It's like she's looking for someone else, maybe someone alive, or like she's trying to get to where she belongs. I keep meaning to ask Sam if he knows her story. It's kind of weird I haven't seen him tonight. He sounded like he would be back by now. He's super sweet, dresses like a pirate and hoards pieces of broken stained glass, coffin nails and other cemetery bric-a-brac so he can create pieces such as this." she said, gesturing to, and then taking the necklace from Jane to tie it around her neck. "Though it can be a little difficult to get a pirate to part with his hoard, luckily Sam likes me. Anyway, I brought you here because I find this the most magical and beautiful of all the cemeteries in this city, it inspires me, I've even written about the girl."

"Really? I'd love to see her and this place from your eyes. The stained glass in your room, is that her?"

"Yes, it is, and I can recite what I've written for you as we walk. It is one of the few things that has imprinted itself in my brain."

"Ok." Jane said, smiling.

Fay stood, reaching her hand out to help Jane up. They cleaned up their little picnic, Fay leaving their stuff next to the tomb, and they walked on through the cemetery together on this cloudy night. Fay began to recite, "The pale girl drifted down the paved, sunlit path. She heard the babbling of brook as the stream creaked, and a duck quacked in the distance. These things no longer affected her. The crow atop the spire watched her, backlit by a clear blue sky. She felt totally at peace walking between tiny plaster and marbled houses, stained glass shining bright."

Just then the moon broke from the clouds lighting up a stained glass window, Jane turned to look as Fay continued her story.

"Stoney people considered her as she idled by on their perpetually cared for and manicured lawns. She continued on until she came to an old but beautiful wrought iron fence. She went through the gate without hesitation and read the names out front. Knocked three times then went in. Never to be seen wandering that path again. She was home and at peace. The door closed forever."

As Fay finished speaking, Jane turned back around and gasped, "Oh my gods they're beautiful."

"What?" Fay said, turning around to face her, puzzled.

"Your wings... I could see them in the moonlight."

"My wi...?" Fay vanished.

Fay found herself standing in her living room feeling

rattled, she noticed immediately that her hands were clenched and her face and neck were ticking. "What the fuck is wrong with me?" she muttered to herself. Then she really took in her surroundings and was even more confused. There was a menagerie of animals in her living room.

"Oh good y'all are back, something has happened." Heck said looking up. "Where's Jane?"

"Still at the Cemetery I assume. I...uh... I kinda freaked out. What's going on? What do you mean something's happened?"

"According to the urgent message that just clacked out of the typewriter, we have a reaper taking souls of the living."

"What? Who?" Fay asked, feeling more and more disorientated.

"Wolf."

"What the actual fuck? No way..."

"There's a witness. FlotSam, the taphofae..."

"We all know Sam." Fay said agitated, "I wondered why I hadn't seen him tonight."

Heck continued to brief her, "Yes, sorry Fay, of course

we do, I've just been reading off the paper. He said he saw a shaggy dog come out of the shadows and approach a woman as she turned to the dog, the dog morphed into Wolf. Sam saw him take the soul of the young woman leaving Pierre's, with a bag of food. He grabbed her, kissed her soul out of her, spit it in his soul bag, took the woman's food and let her drop to the ground. Sam said she slumped to the ground glass eyed and looking 20 years older. No one would recognize her as the same woman that had just walked out. Sam is now hiding on The Otherside, afraid for his life."

"Fuck." Fay said, "The homeless around the city… outside Commander's… fuck!"

"Yeah, we need to find Jane, this is serious."

Fay, Heck, and Ebisneezer portaled back to Metairie to look for Jane. Ebisneezer immediately put his whiskers forward trying to sense her, he sneezed and said, "I cannot sense her soul here, this is very bad." He scanned the cemetery.

Fay closed her eyes, forcing her mind to clear, and

reached out sensing the energy of the cemetery until she felt the wrongness, and almost doubled over. Her eyes flew open and without a word she took off at a dead run toward the Angel of Grief. There spotlit by the moon was the limp body of Jane, laid out on the steps leading into the angel's tomb. Fay apprehensively made her way to the broken form of the woman she loved, yes loved, she knew that now. As Fay carefully picked her up in her arms, her head lolled and her glassy, unseeing eyes seemed to bore into Fay's soul, breaking her heart. She whispered, "I am so sorry." Tears spilled from her eyes as her translucent wings wrapped around them and she blinked out of the cemetery.

Fay landed hard in her own bedroom, almost collapsing under the weight of it all. She didn't collapse though. She walked very carefully as her wings retracted and became completely invisible once more, laying Jane in her bed. As soon as she covered Jane with the blankets she fell to her knees and bellowed a banshee scream as if foretelling the death of all humankind, when in fact it was she who was dying inside.

Claire padded in quietly next to Fay and rubbed her face on hers, "Is she…" she whispered.

"No… but she's not her either. He took her soul with extreme force."

"This is not your fault." She whispered.

"It is, I shouldn't have left her alone. I need to know how to fix this. It has to be fixable." She sobbed.

"I don't know what happened, and you don't have to…"

"She saw my wings and I panicked like a fucking coward, and he stole her from me." She forced out through sobs as she broke down on the floor.

Just then, two small glows followed by two cats appeared on the bed. Heck stared wearily at Fay as Ebisneezer looked over Jane. Heck spoke softly, "This is not your fault. Do not argue. This isn't over, we can and will get her back, but you need to calm down and pull yourself out of this pile of self-loathing. You had an honest reaction to the shock of someone seeing, well… all of you. She has broken something loose inside you. Ebs and I saw your wings wrap around you and Jane as you disappeared from the cemetery. It was astonishing. You, my dear, are so much stronger than you realize. We WILL get her back. Do you understand me, halfling?"

Fays' tears dried and her face set with resolve, "Yes, I hear you." Fay looked at Heck then, "Find and bring Sara. I want every protective ward placed in and around this house. Ask her to bring curtains to enclose the bed, I want Jane to feel as safe as possible." Fay said, trying to keep the tears from falling again.

Heck nodded and was gone. Fay slowly picked herself up off the floor and headed for the living room looking back to stare at Jane's limp form in her bed. Ebisneezer was curled up protectively on the pillow next to her head, he looked up just then and said," I will keep her safe, if for some reason we have to portal out of here, I will make sure you know where we are. I promise you that."

Fay gave a slight nod and headed to the living room. She all but collapsed in her oversized chair and looked around. Bran and Merla perched in their usual spot on the mantle. The grims looked grave, Nubs sat very stoic on the couch, Claire sat almost as still as a statue next to Fay's chair. Fay absently petted Claire while they waited for Heck and Sara. She sensed the portal in her room, and Heck padded in.

"Sara is here, she is going to clean Jane up and check her physical status. Once she does that she will get the curtains up and will be with us shortly."

Sara walked in a few moments later, bent over to hug Fay with red rimmed eyes, and she knelt in front of her and said, "Physically she is ok, or at least she will mend. She's got a lot of bruising, some lacerations, a couple broken ribs and a broken wrist. He probably had to break her wrist to stop whatever spell she was working because it back burned in her palm when it was broken." She paused until Fay looked at her, "Hey. We will get her back."

Fay nodded slightly and Sara sat on the couch. "What do we know?" Fay asked, rubbing her face.

"Not much. The other reapers in his team stopped by while y'all were gone. They are trying to track him. It would seem that they were unaware of his abilities to morph into a dog." Bran relayed.

"Great. Knowing that, I'm pretty sure he's been following us. I've seen a lot of strays around which isn't unusual but it would also be a great way to blend in if you're stalking someone. I also think he's infiltrated my dreams. Goddammit!"

"Do you think I should take her to Ash." Sara asked quietly.

"No!" Fay all but barked and then, "Sorry, no. It's possible he followed us to Austin. I don't want to risk leading him to Ash."

Just then the mail slot opened, and a letter fell to the floor. Outside they heard a howl of laughter followed by an eerie silence.

"That son of a bitch!" Fay yelled as she flew at the door and swung it open. "You fucking coward!" She screamed into the darkness. She slammed the door shut and picked up the piece of paper on her floor. It read:

Hello Lass,

It would seem that you now truly see me as I have now truly seen you. It took you long enough to figure it out, and it took a goddamn taphofae, I guess I got sloppy after all these years. Katrina really was the best cover for my passion, all those missing and homeless, let's just say there would have been far fewer had I not sucked their souls right out of them as I did your girlfriend. Don't worry I'll take real good care of her. This pandemic would have been great cover too if you hadn't gone poking around at the cemeteries. And if it hadn't been for that loudmouth faery, he should have been in his cemetery. When I find him, I will rip his wings from his back and eat them in front of him before reaping his soul.

As for you, your wings will look so beautiful on display with your soul, when I reap it, and I will! I've wanted your soul from the first time I met you as a child, the first time Marie introduced us outside St.Louis #1. You were so young and already so wounded. Now that the cat, well the wolf is out of the bag, the hunt is on. I will meet you where your grief has lain.

-Cairn O'Bogwolf

Fay read the letter aloud with disgust. Upon finishing she crumpled it up and threw it on the table. Fay shook her head and sighed, "Well, it's very clear he's never watched a movie in his miserable life, or he wouldn't lay everything out like that. Secondly, eww, what older man craves the soul of a child. I really can't deal with the awfulness of this letter right now. What I know is that he wants me and Sam. I know Sam is scared and this won't help, but we need him to come back. Heck, I think you're the only one that can convince him."

"I'm on it, Fay."

"Sara, please add any wards to the house you see fit; this house isn't really set up for company, but I have an air mattress we can set up out here or in the master."

Sara nodded," Ok, we can set it up out here. I want to be close but you need your space." She walked off with a small bag and started addressing the doors and windows.

"Ok, for now I think we need to rest. Grims, can you help me pull this chair into my room?"

The grims both approached and pushed on the chair with their heads as Fay pulled, stopping at the side of her bed where Jane lay. Fay curled up in the chair with her notebook, staring at Jane.

Sara cautiously approached and knelt next to her. "Hey." She whispered, "You are the only one blaming yourself for this. Not your team, not her team, not me. Ebs and I decided it would be best to put her body in a static state, it will help her body heal and cause the least amount of trauma due to the attack and separation."

Fay's eyes leaked and she nodded once. Sara touched her back briefly. "You need sleep. I'm here if you need anything." She moved to leave the room.

Fay barely whispered, "Thank you." Then took out her notebook.

March 17

There really are no words.

I kissed Jane tonight, I would have said it to be life changing had the rest of the night not happened

She's gone and I don't know if I can get her back...

I'm staring at the limp, bruised, soulless form of the woman I love.

I wish now that I had told her.

Hindsight.

Her neck is so bruised, I can see the asshole's fingers printed in her skin. Her lip is split and swollen. Her face is so pale and blank and older looking somehow. Her beautiful, calming, green eyes are too calm, cold and distant now. When I picked her up from outside the tomb of the Angel of Grief, I thought for a moment that she was dead, and I nearly died in that moment, I think a part of me has. Her nails are broken, her palm has a weird pattern imprinted in it, Sara thinks she must have gotten a spell off and that he had to break her wrist to break the spell and that's why there are marks on her palm.

She clearly fought him hard.

She must have been so scared. Goddammit!

This is my fault, she saw my wings! SHE SAW ME!!! ALL OF ME!!! And I acted like a child and panicked.

No human, not Marie, not even another banshee has ever seen them clearly.

I was so shocked, and my fight or flight kicked in.

Flight, oh the irony in that.

If I hadn't left, this wouldn't have happened.

I will end him, even if it kills me.

It cannot feel any worse than the pain coursing through me now.

I haven't been able to stop the facial tics and muscle spasms for more than brief moments while focused on a task.

It all hurts so bad I want to rip away this skin, but alas I tattooed these arms to ensure I wouldn't try that again.

I have failed her.

I have failed everyone.

I have failed myself.

Everyone is trying to make me feel better about what happened, but

I know that because of my cowardice Jane was dealt a fate worse

than death, and it's unforgivable.

I will never forgive myself.

-FF

The Eighteenth of March

In the wee hours of the morning Heck peeked in the bedroom, curtains drawn back on the side where Fay was sitting in the oversized chair leaned forward across the bed reaching out towards Jane. Her hair in a rat's nest of a bun on her head and her wings, though not solid, drooped on either side of her. In that vulnerable moment she looked so much like the angel of grief statue that Heck almost cried out for her. Heck held her tongue and jumped up on the back of the chair and curled up and slept.

Fay knew she was in a dream but seemed unable to wake from this particular hellscape. She was Emelyn, the Angel of Grief, slumped over staring at Jane's lifeless body and she was screaming in outrage and frustration, but no one could hear her because she was stone. Then something in her head spoke, "If you could just stop screaming for a moment, I could be of help to you."

Fay stopped her frantic attempts to free herself and listened. "I am Emelyn, you are not me, and neither of us is helpless. We all know who you are, what you are, and we all feel your connection to us. Seek my help in the waking hours, daughter of death, and I shall grant it."

Fay begrudgingly woke as the sun rose, she felt like every part of her was dying as she looked at Jane. Heck felt Fay begin to move and padded down the chair and sat on the arm next to her.

"Did you reach Sam?" Fay asked while she tried to get her swollen eyes to focus on her cat.

"I did. He agreed to come. I'm going to pull him through the portal straight into this house and have promised to escort him anywhere he needs to go. I hope that's ok with you. All of the taphofae have gone into hiding, but Dartanya, Duckie, and

Ellis have all said they will help if they can."

"Good, I think I know what to do but I will need everyone's help. I expect you to guard Sam. I know they have their own glamours and such but I don't want anyone else to get hurt."

"I hope that includes yourself, halfling." Fay didn't say anything so Heck continued glaring at her, "The taphofae now think with what Sam witnessed that Des was murdered by Wolf."

Fay glared at the name, "Let's get everyone here. I want Sara and Ebs to stay here and guard Jane for sure. Everyone else I need with me. He wants a showdown at the Angel of Grief. That's what the last line of the letter meant, and I plan on fucking giving it to him."

"Fay..." Heck began.

"I know what I'm doing Heck." Fay hissed at the cat, her eyes going as black as Death Herself's for a brief second.

Heck averted her eyes briefly, "Ok, halfling, I am with you. I trust you, you have never given me reason not to." She bumped her head against Fay's very briefly and asked, "Do you want me to bring the faeries?"

"Yeah, I'm gonna go make coffee."

When Fay reached the kitchen, she found Sara there already pouring coffee into a mug. Sara turned the spoon stirring her coffee, both hands on the mug.

"Coffee?" Sara asked.

"Sure." Fay mumbled.

"Here." Sara handed her the mug and turned back to get a new mug, Fay stood there for a moment just watching the coffee stir itself before walking into the living room and plopping on the couch. Sara followed close behind, sitting on the other end of the couch.

"What do you need from me?" Sara asked.

"Protect her."

"Fay, whatever you're planning, I beg you, do not get yourself killed, trying to save her. If she survives soul intact and you're dead... it will destroy her."

Fay didn't quite make eye contact with Sara, "In a perfect world my goal would be for both of us to be intact, or as intact as we can be after all this. Honestly, I'm not really sure of my mortality with my lineage. I didn't really have anyone around to explain it. All I know is that I love her, and I should have told her as much, and now I may never get to."

"You will." Sara said so matter-of-factly, that Fay actually looked into her eyes and nodded once.

Heck returned then with Sam on her back, Dartanya, Duckie and Ellis in tow. The taphofae she knew best were here to help her. "Thank you all for coming. I know you're scared, we all are a little." Fay said, making eye contact with each of them.

Ellis was the first to speak, "Baby girl, ya get what ya give in dis world. Ya have shown us respect an kindness."

"Aye, he's right Fay. As scared as I am seein' what I have, knowin' what he's done to so many, and now yer lady. The desecration he's brought to mine and Des' cemeteries, what we fear he's done to Des, we can't let it stand." Sam finished. The other faeries nodded solemnly.

"Ok, Sam, I need you to take a message specifically to Emelyn, can you do that?"

"Aye." He said as she whispered instructions into his

ear.

"As for y'all," She said, looking at the other faeries, " the rest of the inhabited at Metairie need to be informed , and any of the active spirits need to be on alert. We need eyes, and a little bit of chaos wouldn't hurt." They nodded and she continued, "Please be safe. If anything feels wrong, leave. You too, Sam. I'm sending Heck with y'all. When y'all return with a response, we can continue to plan. He wants a showdown at the Angel of Grief, and he's gonna get it." With that she stood, "I'm gonna shower. I will see all of you soon." Fay walked with effort toward her room and just stood in the doorway and watched, Ebs hadn't moved from Jane's side. He appeared to be asleep, but she knew better. From the living room she heard Duckie shout, "Allons y!" as the faeries disappeared with Heck through her portal, followed by approaching footsteps.

"Fay, I want to go with you. I know you want me here, but Ebs is plenty capable, and I have combat talents which may be invaluable." Sara said.

"I don't know, we can talk when everyone is back." She

ripped her gaze away from Jane and retreated to the bathroom, where she proceeded to cry uncontrollably, huddled in the bottom of the shower, clutching herself so tightly that her nails were leaving marks, hair and water streaming down her face and body, steam barricading her from the world. Finally, she pulled herself together enough to bathe, struggling, trying not to scrub off all the pain, misery, and self loathing from her, knowing if she did there would be no skin left. She unwillingly shut off the water and retrieved a towel for her hair and one for her body. Now all wrapped up she quietly made her way out of the bathroom and into her room to find clothes. She immediately noticed Sara sitting with Jane either talking quietly to her or Ebs or both. They both looked at her and Sara began to rise, but Fay waved her down and entered her closet, shut the door, and forced herself not to collapse, as she picked clothes to wear. She finally found underwear, jeans, and a t-shirt that said "I believe in fairies" because why not antagonize a psychopath. She came out of the closet to find Sara gone and Heck sitting outside the door.

"I thought you came out ages ago."

"Yes, this is a time for jokes." Fay glared.

"Says the one wearing the let's enrage a bigoted, soul stealing, murderous fuck head t-shirt." Heck dead panned.

Fay smirked ever so slightly, "Is everyone back?"

"Yeah, shall we convene in the living room?"

"Yeah, give me a couple minutes and I'll be there."

March 18

This may be my last entry.

Whether I survive or not is of no consequence to me.

Especially if I can't get her soul back.

He will suffer though.

If I die, it will be of a broken heart.

-FF

Fay finished writing, slid her notebook under the bed, and kissed Jane's forehead before walking to meet everyone in the living room. In the living room there was one witch, one cat, two crows, two grims, and four taphofae.

"Sam, how did the meeting with Emelyn go?"

"It went well. She can be counted on. While we were there speaking to the inhabited, we also unlocked many of the tombs in case hiding places are needed."

"Good. I assume that includes Emelyn's tomb" Fay said, pacing. She looked at the fae who nodded. "He wants this to all go down there, and now that she is on board I am more than happy to oblige him. We know he's an alterdog, and we assume he will try to scent for me specifically. So, let's wreak a little havoc. Everyone is going to wear at least one item belonging to me. While we are still here Ebs and Heck are going to spread items throughout the cemetery placing articles on some of the inhabited. I trust you and Sam discussed where to place things?"

"Yes." Heck said.

Fay hesitated and looked at Sara, "I don't want to ask this of you, but if you're willing, I will put you in an outfit of mine to confuse him further. This will make you more of a target than any of the rest, other than myself. If you're not comfortable with this we can figure something else out."

"I'm in, I do have a question though."

"Shoot." Fay said.

"That's my question actually, I have silver dipped bullets for my .22s that I carry, will that make a difference on an alterdog?" She asked, pulling out a box filled with bullets. Fay just gaped at her for a moment and then looked at her companions for an answer.

"I have no idea, but it can't hurt, and that's quite clever." Heck said, looking at Sara.

"Well, when you realize you're a witch with real powers, it just makes sense to assume other things are real as well." Sara shrugged. "Also, even if the silver doesn't work, I can enchant them to show his location even if I only graze him with one, the wound will give off a green smoke."

"Very good. We will keep watch over Jane and start dressing the grims and faeries, while y'all spread my wardrobe through the cemetery." She said looking at Heck.

Bran landed on her shoulder. "What shall we do?"

"Be our eyes from above, if you spot him, call out and dive as safely as you can, so we have an idea of his location. If you can get close enough to CAW directly in his ears that would be fantastic."

"Okay, but if I can get that close I'm going to put my beak so far into his eyeball that I can sever it and eat it while he watches with the other one. It's just been that kind of week." Bran cawed, "We will head out now so we can report back when he shows."

Ebs, Heck, Bran, and Merla all disappeared into Heck's portal all carrying an article of clothing. Heck and Ebs would be back soon for more things. Sara jumped in the shower to use Fay's shampoo and body wash to further her disguise. Fay headed for the closet to start dressing the teams for battle. Fay pulled out a My Favorite Murder sweatshirt and placed it over Claire's head and helped her get her front legs through. Claire beamed at her. She wrapped a dignified plaid scarf around the neck of Nubs. She gave each taphofae a hair tie. After her shower Sara perused Fay's closet finally deciding on a

"Fuck the Patriarchy" shirt, a brimmed hat, cuffed jeans that were definitely not hers, and her hip holsters.

Ebs and Heck appeared, Ebs made his way to the bed as Heck rubbed herself on Fay's leg soaking her scent in.

"We're set, and I believe he's there." Heck said.

"Ok." Fay breathed. "Please be careful. When we land, we scatter. Heck, stay with Sam. He and I are the main targets, but he will take anyone out who gets in his way. Sara is going to lead him away from the Angel of Grief and I am going to lead him towards it, throw him off. Once he reaches the Angel of Grief NO ONE is to interfere. No one." She made eye contact with the assembled group.

Everyone nodded but Heck gave her a look. "Halfling. You better heed your own advice and be careful. You are needed here among the living. Remember that."

Fay nodded, and everyone but Ebs left the room. She walked over to her bed, mostly shrouded by curtains, bent low, grasping Jane's hand, and whispered, "I love you more than life itself, I will fix this, or die trying." She kissed Jane's cheek, never making eye contact with Ebs.

The group landed in the middle of Metairie Cemetery, and everyone immediately scattered by land and air. Sara wove in and out of tombs as statues seemed to turn and watch. Fay took off in the opposite direction. The taphofae flitted in and out of the tombs all except for Sam. He rode Heck's back as they jumped from tomb to tomb. The grims began tracking the alterdog.

"Come out you fuckin' faery." They heard him howl, "I know what you're doing and it won't work. Ow! Fuck." The deranged reaper looked up to see three faeries and two crows dropping stones on him. When Wolf looked up, Bran immediately dove for his face, making an otherworldly *CAW CAW CAW* sound as he dove. The panicked reaper immediately shifted into a dog running into the shadows, but not before Bran made contact with his face ripping his talons across his nose before the dog slunk bleeding into the shadows.

Sara ran up the stairs and crouched in the open

doorway of a giant pyramid to listen to the night around her. She was hidden from view when the giant Sphinx next to her turned its head slightly to look at her, "He's coming. In my periphery. Straight ahead of you," It said.

"Thank you." She mouthed and silently began to walk into view.

She could see a dog morphing back into a man with every advancing step, and ranting, "I smell you! I know you're here." As soon as he caught her movement, he launched himself with a snarl, morphing.

Sara already had her guns drawn and hammered back releasing a round from each. Both hit, one in the front foot and one in the opposite back leg. The dog screamed in rage and agony as he transformed back into human form mid air, taking Sara to the ground. He was so stunned to find himself on top of an unknown woman smiling sardonically at him. "What the... doesn't matter..." and he went to kiss her as she struggled to get her hands free. Just then a growl penetrated the darkness followed by teeth, two sets of snarling teeth. Wolf immediately jumped up and transformed, lunging at the first dog, wearing a scarf. Sara grabbed her guns from the ground and rolled the opposite way. Wolf grabbed Nubs by the throat, taking him to the ground forgetting about Claire. Claire stalked the two tumbling beasts, Nubs was pinned, and right as Wolf went to make the kill, Claire leaped and bit him in his back, silver riddled, bleeding leg. Sara and the grims clamored to their feet and ran into the shadows, as the green smoke slowly trailed upward showing his location. The angry deranged reaper pulled himself up glaring at his smoky wounds and cursed.

"You fucking coward. You bring your friends to attempt to do what you can't." His voice echoing off the tombs.

Fay glared into the darkness having heard the shot, angry that he seemed to be reading her mind, "It's not my fault you're a stupid mutt that can't track the correct scent. I've been waiting right here for you the whole time. Right where you wanted me. It's not my fault that you have poor tracking skills you half whit mongrel." He howled with rage and began running in a wide arch around where he knew her to be, green smoke trailing behind him. Fay smiled slightly at his rage and waited, watching the smoke trail that he was clearly oblivious to. She stood on the very same steps where she had picked Jane up from 24 hours earlier waiting for him to make his grand reveal. She rolled her eyes at his clear narcissism as he appeared on a grassy hilled tomb.

He walked languorously down the hill of the Army of Tennessee Tomb. He had a smarmy look on his face though he was bleeding from his nose, hand, and leg, green smoke surrounding him. He was clean shaven, raw pink fleshy patches on his face. "Hello lass, this is just too poetic."

"Is it though or is that just a poorly staged fantas..." she had begun to say but He was upon her quick, as she ultimately knew he would be. In a blink of an eye, he had her by the throat with such force she struggled to stay upright. She clawed at his hands on her neck and tried to knee him, but as she did, he shifted her weight, pulling her closer as if to kiss her, he took a deep breath, and when he did long black smoky tendrils began to pour from her mouth. Fay could barely think or feel, but she knew if she didn't act, she would lose herself, and more importantly Jane forever. She cleared her mind as best she could and with him on her, she forced her weight back as hard as she could slamming into the closed doors of the tomb breaking them open and slamming her back and head into the base of the Angel of Grief. She lay limp, eyes open, and unmoving. The gleam in Wolf's eyes were something to behold. The look of triumph and hunger as he stalked toward her. Fay, for her part, stared unblinking at him, laying as still as a corpse, bleeding from the back of her head. She quite enjoyed the moment his triumph was replaced with surprise and fear as he was lifted up by his lapels, and couldn't help but give him a small smile before he was forced to look away. In all the fracas Wolf failed to notice the movement of the Angel of Grief who no longer looked grief-stricken, but filled with fury.

"I am Emelyn, known to most only as the Angel of Grief, and I will not allow you to disrupt and desecrate my tomb again!" She bellowed. Her stone eyes then turned hollow and black smoke poured out of them as a new voice came through, echoing off the mausoleum walls. "You dare steal while in service to me, Death Herself? You dare kill faeries knowing that I myself am a faery? You steal the soul of an active banshee and you dare to try to steal the essence of one born of my own essence? Are you so arrogant to believe you could do this? That I would not notice? How dare you!! How dare you steal the souls of the living, of others who are in service to me, and attempt to do the same to my daughter!" As she exhaled out the word daughter, she inhaled deeply separating his soul clean from his body and into herself. She tossed the body to the side and picked up Fay. "My dearest one." Death Herself said, standing Fay up. Fay realized then that she could stand on her own and stood up straighter. "Dearest one." Death said again. The statue placed her hands on Fay's face. "You make me proud." She said, stroking her face. Fay's eyes began to well and tears slowly rolled down her face, "You have proven yourself worthy of all things, especially these."

As the word "these" was said Fay felt a solid weight on her back. She looked back to see her wings, velvety bat wings with silver veins running through them. Opening them fully she could see the leathery underside and just how vibrant the veins shown. She collapsed into the statue's arms, weeping.

"I am sorry I kept them bound for so long. I was afraid

once they started to grow they would cause trouble for you in this realm, not realizing how much of yourself I was denying you. Still, I needed to make sure you would be strong enough to glamour and veil them on a day to day basis. I know now you are more than capable." She said holding Fay and stroking her hair.

"Thank you." Fay sobbed into the statue she continued to cling to.

"Look at me." The statue said gently. Fay stood straight again, and looked at her, Fay's eyes now as black and smoky as her mother's, and adjusted herself naturally to balance her wings. "We are not done here." With that she flung a stone hand toward the prone body that had been Wolf. Two small satchels flew from inside his jacket and into the stone hand. One satchel she immediately inhaled. "Those were the souls he was supposed to reap, these were his trophies." She stared into the bag and pulled out a small orb. "This is Jane, take her back to her body. I will dispatch the rest of your teams to return these to as many bodies as they can." Fay nodded once, unfurled her wings, veiled herself and took to the sky for the first time, tears burning as they streamed down her face.

Death watched her go before turning to the other harbingers that had appeared from the shadows upon her call. "Please find the bodies that these souls go to, if they have no host left bring them to me. Please see that they are helped with reuniting and integrating back into society. This is on me, and I will see things set right. Also, please see that the corpse is removed from Emelyn's home, I care not where it ends up as long as it's not here. He has desecrated this place enough without rotting here too. Fay is tending to Jane, as it should be." Anubis lumbered forward carefully, taking the satchel from the statue's hand. Death bent down and kissed him on the head and said "thank you Nubs, but do lighten up." She grinned and with that the eyes turned back to stone and Emelyn slowly laid back down to continue her vigil of grief.

Fay landed on her own stoop, unveiling herself except the wings, she stood there for a moment forcing her eyes back to blue, and then opened the door. The house was empty, everyone out on errand, except Ebisneezer, he would be with Jane. She walked through the house, though relatively small, it felt like a mile from her front door to her bedroom. She walked slowly and deliberately. She rested her head on her closed bedroom door before taking a deep breath and opening it. Ebisneezer turned his head to look at her.

"I've got her." Fay said, barely above a whisper. She showed him the orb.

He sighed with relief and said, "I will leave you two alone and go help the others. I heard the call."

"Thank you." Fay said as she sat on the edge of the bed allowing the veil to drop and her wings to spread. One drooping on to the floor and the other splayed across the bed and partially covering Jane.

Ebs made a small meowing sound that sounded like wow, as he disappeared through the door.

Fay swiped at the unwelcome tears rolling down her face as she stared at Jane. She slowly bent her head down next to Jane's ear and whispered, "Please wake up...please be you." As more tears fell from her face to Jane's. She sat up, very gently opened Jane's mouth and held the orb close. It turned smoky and tendrils made their way into Jane's mouth and nose. Fay sat there quietly stroking Jane's face and hair.

Without warning Jane sat up gasping and grasping at her, the first coherent word was, "Fay?" It came out frantic and hoarse.

Fay held Jane by the shoulders and said, "I'm here Jane. I'm here, please just look at me."

Jane focused her eyes then, calming as Fay's tear filled face steadied. "Fay, what's wrong? What's happened? Why are you covered in blood?" Jane immediately grabbed her in a hug. "Fay, it's ok. I'm ok . What's wrong?"

Fay lifted her head and whispered, "I'm so sorry. I shouldn't have left you there. I didn't mean to leave." Fay felt like an asshole, she didn't mean to unburden herself this way, but she was so mixed up with the flood of guilt and relief, it just came out.

"Sorry for leaving me where?" And then she tensed, remembering.

Fay hugged her tighter, "Don't go back there if you're

not ready, and if you want me to leave, I will." She began to pull away, but Jane stopped her.

"Please don't. I need to remember. What happened is not your fault. I didn't even realize what I had said until you were gone. I was so mad at myself for blurting that out and then there was this large dog, and then it wasn't a dog. It was Wolf, and he… he …" she tensed again and felt her own face and neck which had already begun healing. Then she trailed her hands down Fay's fresh bruises and matted bloody blond hair. "He grabbed me by the throat, I grabbed his face and blasted him with my magic which burned part of his beard at the root, kinda like Nair. He let go of my throat for a second, long enough to break my wrist severing the magic, but I was already oxygen deprived by the time he let go… he was right back on me again, I remember clawing at his face, and him kissing me, and then nothingness. My brain is relaying messages from my body to my soul on what happened while they were separated." She drooped a little and said, "I need to ask you something sensitive, and I need you to promise you won't blink out."

"Anything." Fay said tentatively.

"Am I seeing your wings? Or is this some hallucination of the ordeal I've been through?"

Fay smiled a little self consciously and said, "Oh no, you're seeing them. And I'm not going anywhere if you don't want me to."

"I don't. I know, or am knowing if that makes sense, what you did to get me back. I know what you were willing to sacrifice, I know you spent every moment that you weren't planning, holding my hand and talking to me. Like I said my brain retained all that, even though I was not whole. I know you love me. And I love you, but know this, if your little suicidal crusade had gotten you killed and I had become whole, I would have learned necromancy to bring you back just to kill you myself for what you put me through by not being here. I wouldn't have felt whole without you. Now, I want you to hold me against your chest and wrap those magnificent wings about us both."

Fay was taken aback by all this, and it took her brain a few moments to catch up. When it did she gave her bloodied and bruised self a once over, deciding in a mere second that this moment was more important than a shower. Without saying a word, she briefly let go of Jane, shifting so she was behind her and beckoned for her to lay back. As Jane did velvety leather wings encased them both and they slept.

The Nineteenth of March

March 19

Today I am the happiest I've ever been.

I have more than I dreamed possible.

The last two days were damn near impossible and wouldn't have been possible without friends in literally all shapes and sizes.

I woke sometime in the wee hours with Jane wrapped against me, both of us cocooned in the safety of my wings. (My wings! My wings! That alone is liable to cause me to burst into tears again.) I slipped out of the bed, careful not to wake Jane. I had to get the blood, dirt, and memories that coated my skin off. I ran a bath; I was still too tired to stand. I was rinsing my blond hair in a sea of red when I heard the door open and Jane shuffle in sleepily. We just couldn't be apart. She didn't really say anything, just sat bundled up in a blanket on the toilet and waited until I was finished. As I toweled off, she dried my hair, and we both went back to bed.

About midmorning the crew brought us coffee and Danishes in bed, everyone shared their point of view of the events. I also let the teams know that after this debriefing of events that Jane and I are to be left alone for the next 24 hours and if I catch so much as a whisker coming through the closed door or wall that I will kill them myself. There were no arguments.

Jane's eyes got so big when Sara told us about her near miss with the bastard, and how she shot him! I am really glad to know her, and I look forward to meeting the others chosen by Ash. Sara is going to take care of McMortem's while Jane convalesces here with me.

The grims are on much friendlier terms after Claire saved Nubs'... well, nub last night. I was already gone but apparently Death Herself told him to lighten up. That amuses me thoroughly.

It was confirmed that Des was murdered by that maniac. The story is so horrible. Apparently he had been hiding his hoard of souls there for years in the old crematorium, when Des started talking to me about things, Wolf felt he had to go because I would poke around, which I did. That night when we came. Wolf had removed his hoard and trapped poor Des in there, burning him alive; he didn't even do him the courtesy of reaping his soul first. So disgusting.

The teams were able to get most of the recent souls back to their bodies, unfortunately a few had expired, and all the older ones, the ones from Katrina had all expired. It sickens me and will haunt me for a long time. I thought I knew him. He has left deep mental and physical scars upon us and this city. It is unforgivable, the things he did.

For the first time my mother has spoken directly to me and indirectly laid hands on me. I am so filled with emotion, I never really appreciated how hard it must be for her. She bound my wings to protect me, not realizing how much of myself I was being denied. (I guess that makes her a helicopter parent) Apparently not just my wings have been bound but other faery abilities too. I have some kind of sight that has shaken loose as well. I haven't really looked much, I'm not ready. I know my eyes shift to smoky black, no iris, no pupil but I can see...I see too much now I think... BUT SERIOUSLY its creepy as fuck. It's like her eyes. I don't know what it means.

While a touch of hurt and anger still flare. I understand that her intent was good.

To be told by Death Herself, mother or not, that she is proud of you is an overwhelming moment.

But again being her daughter there is a little hurt and anger there... 33 years and now you're proud?!?

Anyways.... I'll deal with my mommy issues later... today is not that day...

Because there's Jane. Both of us have some serious traumas from this experience that we will need to work through. But at least we have each other which is more than either of us realized before this mess. Now that I have her, I have no intentions of ever letting go.

Things learned:

1. Even if you can't see the end game. Love always wins. Always.

2. Talking cats are overrated. Heck went and told Marie what all transpired, now I'm in trouble and she expects to "officially"

meet Jane on my birthday.

What I plan to learn in the immediate future:

1. Whether threats work on my housemates

2. Whether me and these wings of mine will fit in the

shower with Jane.

-FF

Epilogue:

The Thirty-First of March

March 31

Tomorrow is my 34th birthday.

Tomorrow the two most important women in my life will meet

officially. Nothing stressful about that.

I actually think Jane's way more worried.

It's not like they've never met; it was just like 15 years ago or so.

I picked up Commander's tonight to have for birthday lunch

tomorrow, I think Marie would disown me if we didn't have

Commander's for my birthday.

Jane and Heck have seemed awfully secretive. They're in CAHOOTS,

cahoots I tell ya!! I know they're up to some shenanigans… I hate shenanigans, well at least I do when I'm not part of them, or rather the probable subject of them.

The nightmares are lessening which I am thankful for. Sara created a tincture to help facilitate dreamless sleep. It helps, but sometimes things just claw through. I know her and Jane have also been taking it. Our physical wounds healed nice and quickly, the mental and emotional damage lingers somewhat.

I still refuse to SEE, I fear it will bring more nightmares. I have at least been able to keep them from shifting so much.

I haven't been back to Metairie, it's too much, it's haunted now. Sam has come by a few times to check on me, and bring me little pieces of glass and things trying to cheer me up. He's such a sweet faery.

At least Jane and I have each other now.

That matters the most.

At least we stopped being so foolish.

Foolish

Fool

Fuck

I can't believe tomorrow is my birthday

Cue dramatic introspection

Yes, I know it's coming... especially after all that's happened.

You try being birthed of death and not have some major introspection on your birthday, unknown nonexistent person I'm having a one-sided argument with.

-FF

The First of April

Fay woke to a kaleidoscope of colors streaming across her room, she turned over, wings retracted in their veiled state, to find the spot next to her cold and empty. She looked at the rose she had given Jane for her birthday flourishing on the opposite nightstand. She sighed. Just then she could hear footsteps approaching along with the scent of coffee and something sweet. She turned back to face the door.

"Good morning, my favorite fool. Happy Birthday!" Jane kissed her as the tray with coffee and bananas foster French toast hovered and gently set itself on Fay's lap.

"Thank you! What a wonderful way to wake up, though I wish you wouldn't call me a fool."

"Well, I hope you don't waste your birthday wish on something so... well... foolish. You will always be my fool, not just because your birthday is April first, but also for being fool enough to love me, fool enough to come for me against the odds."

"Foolish not to see what we have. Foolish enough to leave you ..." she broke off.

"Don't do that. First, we both dragged our feet when it came to us. Secondly, you are the only one upset with you. The rest of us are so very proud. I love you, Fay Fool Finis." She kissed her and bounded away calling back. "Come on, we've got plans. Marie will be here soon and I'm freaking out."

"Jane Heather McMortem! That is NOT my middle name!" She yelled, smiling despite herself.

Fay finished her breakfast, enjoying every bite. She slowly made her way to the bathroom to shower and had a mild panic attack about the convoluted nature of her birth, and about Marie's visit. Marie or, Mama Marie as she called her as a child and still sometimes did, is the only maternal figure she's had; Marie's feelings about Jane were important. Then the flashbacks of Jane's birthday flew through her consciousness and she crumpled, smokey eyed, shaking, sitting in the bottom of the shower, wings drooping.

Fay heard the bathroom door creak open quietly, and Jane approached as if sensing her trepidation.

"Can I join you?" She asked quietly.

"Of course." Fay smiled slightly at her voice and shifted bringing her wings in tightly so there would be room.

Jane slipped her clothes off and stepped into the shower. "What's wrong?" Jane asked, crouching and caressing her wings.

"Just stressed, birthday, Marie, just all the things." Fay said not looking up.

"Oh, you so do not get to be stressed about Marie! That's my job." She laughed. "As for your birthday you better learn to love it because I have plans. Now look at me with those smoky eyes you always try to hide." As Fay looked at her, Jane kissed her and whispered, "Stop hiding from me, I want to see all of you." She kissed her again, stood, rinsed off, and left Fay gaping after her as water beat across her body. Jane peeked back around the corner, "and as for my birthday, if that's what you meant by all the things. It was the best birthday of my life. You finally acted the fool that you are and kissed me; that's all I had wanted, you." She winked and disappeared. Fay continued to stare, thinking to herself, how does she do that? How does she know what I'm thinking? She heard in the distance, "It's not witchcraft, we've known each other for more than 15 years, fool." A grin in Jane's voice.

The light in the bathroom changed to a gold for a moment and then Heck was sitting outside the shower. "I know it's your birthday and all, but do hurry. I am portaling Marie here soon, apparently when she retired so did Voodoo, and as much as she loves me, I can only distract her so long when she's on a mission to see you. Especially after recent events."

Fay groaned, still sitting in the shower, "I know. I'm getting out." Fay stood up, turned off the water and walked out of the shower wrapping a towel around her as she went.

"Ok, back in a flash." Heck said with a Cheshire grin, which is even more unsettling on an actual cat.

Just as Fay finished dressing and Jane had dried her hair, there was a bright beam of gold light from the living room followed by a woman's voice. "Chèrie, you best get in here and hug ya' Mama

Marie."

Fay grinned despite herself, "Come on, love.", she said, grabbing Jane's hand.

Jane took her hand a little apprehensively, but her angst eased when she saw the genuine happiness glitter in Fay's eyes. They strode into the living room hand in hand, Fay only breaking her grasp when she reached Marie. Marie was a tall, elegant, older black lady with a mane of gray hair that matched her soft gray eyes. Crow's feet crinkled around those eyes as Fay approached.

"Mama Marie!" Fay said, grasping her. And kissing both cheeks.

"Child, step back and let this ol' lady look atcha fully now."

"You are not old, Mama Marie."

"Child, you an' I both know, that bein' more than a hundred years, makes me more of a winter chicken than a spring one. I mean look at these snowy feathers, Chèrie."

Jane attempted to stifle a choke, but failed. Fay looked

back and grinned, "I know right?She doesn't look a day over 90."

"Ooh, child, I know it's ya' birthday, but I will make it ya' death day too, if ya' don't watch ya' mouth. Now Fay, let me see them in all their glory." Fay unveiled and unfurled her wings using them to pull the older woman closer to her wrapping her in a winged hug. Fay was sure she could feel Marie's tears on her shoulder, but she knew better than to mention it. They broke their embrace and Marie said, "Now, show me the rest."

Fay looked away, "I don't like it."

"Fay, Child, let Mama see." Fay looked at her again, eyes smoky. "Oh child, your eyes are beautiful, I know it's a lot, but I can help when ya' ready." Marie flashed her a smile and her eyes turned smoky for just a second. When Fay gasped, she laughed, and then turned to Jane, "You child, Mama Marie has waited for ya' to come into my little Fay's life fully. Y'all are such fools to have waited so long to love each other. Mama Marie knew the day ya' met that this would come; the Fates, however, enjoy pullin' strings and playing with timelines." Mama Marie kissed both Jane's cheeks and whispered, "I have a feeling you've been waiting for things to line up just as long as I have." Jane's eyes widened briefly as she remembered her own tarot cards. Mama Marie pulled out of the embrace smiling, and said, "Now, Hecate promised me there would be food. Commander's, she said."

Fay rolled her eyes and went to pull the Muffulettas, pecan pie, and turtle soup she had picked up the previous night out of the fridge. They talked and ate the afternoon away. Mama Marie excused herself to take a nap in Fay's bed when Jane approached with a picnic basket and roses.

"Come on." Jane said, reaching her hand out. "I have a surprise for you."

Fay stood grasping her hand and followed her to the portal Heck had opened in the living room, they walked through, Heck too. She wanted to be close if this went south fast. When they landed Fay immediately stiffened. They were standing outside the tomb of Emelyn.

"Please don't freak out." Jane said quickly, seeing Fay's expression. "I brought you here to remind you why you love it so much. You seem to have forgotten its beauty after the incident.

You're letting him win to some degree when you do that, and you aren't showing the proper love and respect to the entities that helped us. I brought you to Emelyn specifically because the flowers are a thank you for her." Jane lowered her voice, "Fay, look at me." She obeyed, so Jane continued, "I am right here, I am not going anywhere, and I love you." She kissed Fay's cheek.

They proceeded into the tomb and thanked Emelyn, and left the dozen red roses. Jane walked her to the exact same spot where they had eaten for Jane's birthday; the only difference was that there were about 100 floating candles dancing around them and the immediate tombs. Jane set up the picnic with the wave of her hand and a few whispered words. They sat very close together on the blanket. Jane placed a small wrapped bundle in front of Fay. She opened her present and immediately started shaking her head. In her hands she held two custom made tapestries, one was the Fool tarot card, Fay with full wings standing on the edge of a cliff, Heck, Bran, and Nubs sitting behind her, and if she's not mistaken what looked like four beetles boring into the patterned edge. Over the cliff that Fay was facing was an outstretched arm the rest out of frame. The tapestry under the Fool card was the High Priestess card.

A tapestry of Jane in full high priestess regalia one of her arms

outstretched and out of frame.

Fay rolled her glistening eyes, "Thank you." she

whispered.

"I told you, you are my fool." Jane smiled.

They kissed then, only stopping when they saw the pale girl start

her journey, trying to find her way home. Watching her, Fay realized

that she had fallen in love with Metairie all over again, and that she

was home with Jane in her arms.

Just as Fay sighed contentedly feeling truly at peace

for the first time since the incident, Heck reappeared and winked at

Jane. Fay looked back and forth between them and glared. "Now

what?"

"One more surprise." Jane whispered into her ear.

"Come on, my fool."

Fay sighed and got to her feet while Jane smirked and vanished

their picnic. Heck created a portal and they all walked through.

They came out right in front of the path leading to Ash. Fay looked at her curiously and Jane grinned. "Did you really think the tree of LIFE wouldn't request your presence on your BIRTHDAY?"

"Well, when you put it in those terms..." Fay said and followed her.

When they reached the clearing, Fay noticed a couple of things immediately. One, her wings had unveiled themselves and her eyes went smoky, and two, there were far more people than she expected, including Marie. She noted that Sara and Marie were engrossed in conversation before everyone stopped to look at her.

"I wanted you to meet the rest of the coven." Jane beamed at her and started to drag her to each person. "This is Jess, they are a tranself." As the elf turned to greet her their masculine features transitioned fluidly to feminine. Fay smiled at the beautiful being as they moved on, "This over here is RR, but you have to say it, arr arr, like a pirate, because she's a pirate witch, most think her a water sign, but she's actually a wind witch."

"My name is Karri." The witch said, rolling her eyes at Jane.

"Yes, and as we agreed Karri is a shite pirate name."

"I didn't agree, you just started calling me RR and it stuck."

Jane grinned evilly at the witch and pulled Fay along, this purrrrfect creature here is Drezden, he's a doll. The dirty white colored, cat like, faery stepped closer inhaling Fay and Jane's breath, in greeting, and nodded slightly. Fay tensed slightly but calmed as Jane squeezed her hand and they continued on, "This is Simon, he surprisingly says little." Simon nodded sagely, but Fay noticed a twinkle in his eye and two sharp incisors as they kept walking. They closed in on two women, one with dark wavy hair the other with hair fierier than Jane's, both had killer cheekbones, the women turned in unison and spoke as one in a Scottish accent, "Hallo lovelies, pleased to finally meet you in the flesh Fay."

"Hello Michelle, Shirley. They are seers and unconventional twins." Fay cocked an eyebrow at her. "It's a long story. Let's just say that their son of a witch of a father liked the ladies… a lot." She said as they moved toward a shorter male with a ridged head and claw-like nails, steam trailed out his nose as he breathed, his irises sparked like golden embers, " this is Aidan, he is Sara's son. He is a dragonkin, which means he is both an eight year old boy and an ageless dragon." He smiled up at them with pointed teeth. Fay looked back at Sara, realizing for the first time that her face looked more angular here, and as their gazes met Sara's eyes were on fire, as she smiled across the clearing at Fay. Still on the move Fay broke eye contact with Sara just in time for Jane to say, "This is Frances." Frances shot her a look. "Sorry, Franny, and Emma." The two older women, one with hair as gray as Marie, greeted them from beneath their wide brimmed hats. Then they approached a man with long wavy graying hair, "This is Frederick, he is a Wolf hybrid. When folklore refers to a werewolf, it's him, essentially. Jane could see Fay struggling not to tense as she shook his hands. Jane was about to say something when Frederick leaned in and whispered, "We are not the same. He and I, his kind, are why my kind struggle with stigma, but I understand your apprehension around me, which is why I stayed in this form, though as you can see

Ash tends to bring out our best features." He smiled warmly at her nodding to her wings, and she smiled shakily back. In that moment she realized she was in control of how much of her true self she could show, or not. It took a little effort, but she was able to will her eyes back to blue, and then she smiled more brightly at Frederick. Fay hadn't realized they had wound themselves all the way to the tree. As they approached Ash, a lanky blond with pointed ears dropped from inside the tree, hanging by her feet from a limb.

"And this magnificent creature is Aud. She's the most amazing aerialist I've seen, with or without wings." Just then Aud laughed, waved, and dropped like a bat swooping into the sky. They watched her acro-bat-ics for a moment before Jane turned to Fay and said, "You hold the seat of honor tonight, my fool." She said gesturing at the one seat sticking out from the tree.

"This is gonna be a thing isn't it? Like you calling...um...Karri, RR?" She asked as she took her seat.

Jane grinned and stood next to her, as they surveyed the group gathered around them. Fay looked around at all the different peoples plus their familiars, she then realized both harbinger teams were present. She caught Marie's smoky eyes and they smiled at each other. This, this was what it was like to have family and she knew, in that moment, she would do everything in her power to protect these beings and this tree.

She felt Ash speak to her more than heard, *welcome to the living Fay, guardian of the coven of the tree of life.*

This book has ended,
but the story remains
in PERPETUAL CARE.

Lake Lawn Metairie Cemetery
New Orleans Louisiana

Lafayette Cemetery #1
New Orleans Louisiana

Saint Roch Cemetery
New Orleans Louisiana

Holt Cemetery
New Orleans Louisiana

*The only image not taken by me, taken by my wife, Heather Horton

Oddfellow's Rest
New Orleans Louisiana

Greenwood Cemetery
New Orleans Louisiana

Oakwood Cemetery
Austin Texas

Oakwood Cemetery
Austin Texas

Acknowledgments

First and foremost, I have to thank my wife, Heather. Without her I probably never would've discovered my love for New Orleans and its cities of the dead. I also have to thank her for never letting me fall as I stumble in and out of portals.

Secondly, I have to thank my cover artist, Amy "Chaos" Dix. When I reached out via social media and asked if she would be interested in creating the cover for my book, I never imagined what good friends we would become. She plucked the image from my brain and made it a reality, and for that I am eternally grateful.

Find her *@sedatrix* on twitter and TikTok (if these are still things when you read this)

At the time of writing this there are only three people other than myself that know how this book ends:

Katy Llewellyn: My friend and fellow writer

http://klewellenwrites.wordpress.com

Richard Hansen: My dad

Dr. Mary Rutledge: My editor extraordinaire

They were the first ones to follow me on this journey, helping with

unfamiliar territory, and editing the fuck out of this book.

Well, not the fuck, there's plenty of F bombs in this book.

Thank y'all for accompanying me, and keeping me on track when I

wavered.

I can be found here: (if these are still things when you read this)

Email: strange.jane.13@gmail.com

Tiktok: @strangejane13

Instagram: strange.jane.13